Wanda stared at the tough young black as if for the first time. He was an ebony-skinned warrior, a gallant and brave native in a strange land, no longer innocent but street-wise. She came at him with nails and teeth, and Lenny laughed as he grabbed her arms and threw her down onto the bed.

"Listen babe, you're a nice lady. But you got one problem. You're white and you think like a white. No white could ever get you into this mess. You wouldn't have let it happen. But you did let it come down with a black man, and that's 'cause you think a black man can't do nothin' more than fuck. You like all whiteys, always lookin' at the color. Can't get past the damn color. Well, it'll cost you this time, Wanda, but maybe you learnin' the most valuable lesson of your life!"

—BLACK IN A WHITE PARADISE

**Other Holloway House Originals
By Amos Brooke**

THE LAST TOKE

DOING TIME

BLACK IN A WHITE PARADISE

by Amos Brooke

An Original Holloway House Edition
HOLLOWAY HOUSE PUBLISHING CO.
LOS ANGELES, CALIFORNIA

Published by
HOLLOWAY HOUSE PUBLISHING COMPANY
8060 Melrose Avenue, Los Angeles, CA 90046
All rights reserved. No part of this book may be reproduced or transmitted in any form or by any means, electronic or mechanical, including photocopying, recording or by any information storage and retrieval system, without permission in writing from the Publisher.
Copyright © 1978 by Holloway House Publishing Company. Any similarity to persons living or dead is purely coincidental.
International Standard Book Number 0-87067-255-X
Printed in the United States of America
Cover illustration by Steve Huston
Cover design by Bill Bergmann

CHAPTER ONE

"MOTHERLESS HOG NEAR DEAD!" Lenny Thompson gritted his teeth, urged the old Caddy into the Magnolia Street exit off the San Diego Freeway. The car sputtered, protesting.

"What you mean *near* dead?" Jason Cribbs' handsome black face cracked wide in a grin.

Lenny scowled sidelong at his friend. The Caddy had brought them from New York across country to Southern California, blowing a muffler and carburetor along the way, and sucking up half their bankroll in repairs, gas and oil. Now it moved like a sister he'd known back East . . . all shimmies, and sharp, tinkling noises. Only the car was not being coquettish. Rather, it was gasping as if it had chosen the Golden State for its burial.

Trembling, the car coughed its way onto a tree-lined street in Fountain Valley. "Nice!" Jason pronounced.

Lenny nodded in agreement. Southern California was nothing like he had ever seen back East . . . all palm trees and neatness and clean. Lord, was it clean! Not like Harlem, no sir. Here, the warm weather seemed to spur folks into upkeep of their property. There were no overturned garbage cans lining the curb, no half-naked black kids playing stick-ball or running tag in the streets. Lenny could readily see why they called it the Golden State.

"Hey, bro, lookie here." Jason pointed to a billboard sign that read *Luxury Apartments—immediate occupancy.*

Lenny squinted through the dirty windshield at the apartment complex. *Palmwood Gardens,* the sign over the entrance door read. The place appeared big enough to accommodate half of New York City and still have room for future migration. He eased the gurgling Caddy to the curb, studied the glass entrance doors speculatively. It was like nothing he had ever seen back East, he thought again: a lifetime dream come true, he and Jason having talked about moving to California since boyhood, and only the fuzz, the man, the heat coming down on their small-time drug-dealing operation back in the Big Apple finally pushing them into turning the dream into reality.

"S'pose them dudes inside ready fo' black folks?" Jason stared questioningly at his friend.

Lenny grinned evilly. He supposed the luxury complex was full of white people, and the idea of crashing their scene, of walking in black and sassy—a Harlem type strut—was almost as good as the thought of the Mexican senoritas that friends who had visited the state repeatedly told him about. "Shit!" he said at last. "Ain't never carried my chocolate behin' where they ready for me, mah man. And you—shit!" He shoved playfully at Jason. "Ain't nobody, no where, no time gone be ready for you!"

Jason pursed his lips in a mock, angry pout. He watched Lenny turn the ignition key to off, laughed along with him when the Caddy trembled and choked in afterburn. "Near dead, mah ass," he mocked his good buddy, the dude who was more like family—and vice versa—than the families both had left back East. "Sucker dead as that white boy done overdosed on them drugs y'all sold 'im, what brought the man down on our case. Car *dead,* man. An' we stranded out here in all this sunshine an' luxury apartment livin'!"

"Hardship sure 'nough make me sad," Lenny jived.

The glass entrance doors to Palmwood Gardens opened on a plush lobby complete with overstuffed armchairs, deep sofas, and a registration desk that would have done justice to a double star-rated hotel. To the left of the entrance stood a recreation room boasting pool tables and a quarter-fed electronic tennis game machine. Next to that stood a door marked *TV Room.* The door was open. Inside, there was row upon row of crushed velvet, sofa type seats that graduated upward like the seats in movie houses. Jason whistled in approval. But Lenny had turned his attention back to the registration desk, was staring at the girl with long dark hair who had noted them when they walked in, and stood, head cocked, as if waiting for them to state their business.

"Can I help you boys?" the girl receptionist said at last.

Jason's wandering gaze settled on the girl. "Sure 'nough a dangerous offer," he said barely above a whisper.

"Best get us a 'partment first," Lenny told him. He moved to the reception desk, leaned forward on his elbows. He grinned widely at the attractive white girl, let his gaze wander leisurely downward over her breasts.

"Lookin' for rooms," he added.

The girl fidgeted, blushed under his bold gaze. "We . . . we have *apartments,*" she said tightly.

Lenny looked hard into her brown eyes. "Do tell."

The girl's blush deepened. "And it's first and last month's rent, a hundred dollars security, seventy-five processing fee and ten dollars key deposit." She paused to sniffle, pull herself up tall. Told *that* nigger, her defiant expression said. "In advance!" she added tersely.

Lenny glanced back over his shoulder to where Jason was toying with the electric tennis game machine, motioned him forward. He watched his friend look from him to the uppity white girl, mentally size up the scene at the desk, then strut, hands deep in his pants pockets, head tilted to one side in super-bad, NYC style. He, too, leaned forward on his elbows on the reception desk. It was his turn to stare boldly at the blushing white girl's jutting tits. The other women—secretaries seated at typewriters in the office-like area behind the desk—had stopped what they were doing, stared with raised brows.

"Say as how we got to guy the place 'fore we moves in," Lenny told Jason.

Jason pursed his lips, looked about the large, plush lobby with the eye of a prospective buyer. He nodded thoughtfully, looked back to the flustered receptionist. "How much?"

"Listen . . .!" the girl fumed. She opened her mouth to add something more, seemed to remember that her job included being cordial to potential tenants. She sniffled again, again pulled herself up tall, and finally added, "A two bedroom furnished will cost you, ah . . . *you boys* three hundred and thirty-nine dollars a month. That's the cheapest apartment we have. It's in the back overlooking the parking lot."

Jason's brows went up. "Got *This Door Used Fo' Deliveries* on it, too?"

The receptionist again opened her mouth to speak, decided against it and clamped her lips tightly shut. Hands on hips, eyes flashing in anger, she glared at them.

Lenny sobered. "What the most *expensive* 'partment y'all got?" he asked, his tone of voice as deadly as the receptionist's expression. "Don't know 'bout no California black folks, but back to New York we go in style . . . you know, mama?"

Another woman, older, wearing rimless glasses and a severe business suit, appeared from the open door to the office behind the receptionist. "Our most expensive rental is on poolside. The balcony overlooks the center court of the complex. It will cost you boys $420 a month. With first and last, the security, the processing fee and key deposit, that will be one thousand and twenty-five dollars to move in."

Lenny glanced sharply at Jason. The other man nodded once. Looking back to the witch who had come to the receptionist's rescue, Lenny said, "We take it!"

The older white woman blinked. The receptionist's mouth dropped open. The secretaries behind the desk stared in amazement. Lenny grinned evilly. "Y'all can put clean sheets on the beds while me an' mah main man here get our bags out the car," he told the white witch. "One thing I can't abide is triflin' maid service."

"The tour is part of the Palmwood service," the white witch with the rimless glasses said in an official voice. She had taken their money, made them fill out a month-to-month lease that required everything except birthmarks, and now, the deal made, she was leading them through the second set of double glass doors, into the center court. The doors opened on an area that reminded Lenny of Miami Beach . . . tall, neatly trimmed palms . . . a pool so big that it boasted an island with a palm tree of its own . . . and then, two wooden bridges over what appeared to be a lilly pond, and an enormous, steaming Jacuzzi beyond that. The place was immense. Far bigger than it had appeared from the street.

"Our pool is kept at a constant 82 degrees," the management lady continued as they followed her down the short flight of concrete steps to the inner grounds. She turned, faced the clubhouse again, pointed. "Upstairs we have a ping pong room with two tables, a shuffleboard area, a golf driving range, separate gyms for our men and women tenants, each fully equipped and with sauna and showers, and lecture rooms where our guest speakers hold seminars, give guitar and dance and yoga lessons, hold bio-feedback sessions and discuss topical issues." The white lady smiled. She looked to them for a reaction.

Jason whistled softly. "Don't never have to leave this place 'cept fo' food."

"We have a fully stocked shopping center around the corner," the white lady quickly added. She smiled in self-satisfaction.

Lenny studied the witch. If she took her hair down from its ridiculous bun, discarded the glasses and wore makeup, she might look human, he decided. The legs beneath the hem of the business suit skirt were well-formed, trim. The wide flare of her hips and the roundness of her buttocks were visible despite the austere outfit, and above thv waist, her breasts were full and high. She might even be foxy if she came off her perch, Lenny amended mentally. She might even be a woman.

"And downstairs," the white lady continued, "we have our fun room." Again she pointed, this time to the glassed-in area directly under the huge clubhouse. "Once a month we hold disco dances downstairs—one dollar admission with bar privileges."

"Now you talkin' New York style," Jason said, smacking his lips, as if in anticipation of the drinks that would be served at the next disco dance.

Lenny was busy studying the white lady, the name plate pinned to the lapel of her suit jacket. *Wanda* it read. He glanced at her left hand . . . no wedding ring! A frustrated bitch, he decided . . . pushing 35, perhaps married and divorced, and concentrating now on "a career" instead of what came naturally.

"We have gas-operated barbecue pits in the downstairs area also," Wanda went on. "They are at your disposal at all times, and on Sunday evening we have a complimentary salad bar, and sometimes side dishes of spaghetti or baked macaroni, and always coffee and sometimes wine. You bring your dinner service, we supply the rest. Most of our tenants bring steaks and char them on the barbecue to go with the salad, and on Sunday morning, *every* Sunday morning, we also have a complimentary continental breakfast." Again she smiled in self-satisfaction, waited for a response.

Jason looked to Lenny, winked. He looked back to Wanda. "Y'all got any black folks here? 'Sides us, what I mean. This place got any color?"

It was Wanda's turn to blush. "Our night security man is, ah . . . is *colored.*"

"Sure 'nough?" Jason persisted.

Wanda studied him a moment, then turned abruptly away. "If you, er . . . if you *gentleman* will follow me, I'll show you to your apartment." She started forward, the canned tour apparently over.

Together, Lenny and Jason followed . . . be-bopping past the large, heated pool where white girls, mostly blondes, lay sunning themselves on adjustable deck chairs. Several glanced curiously their way. One smiled. The others simply stared.

Lenny stared, too. He stared first at the foxy white girls beside the pool, then his gaze returned to the swish of Wanda's wide hips. He pursed his lips. He could imagine the white witch naked, her defenses down, and flustered—no, astounded—by her first look at a nude black man. He had never particularly liked white women . . . too inhibited, not at all like a sister in bed. But Wanda represented a challenge. Almost as much so as the long trip across country in the hog that had died somewhere around Illinois. He followed and thought about how it would be to make the subdued white lady say "uncle."

The apartment was on the second floor, with a balcony that ran the length of the place and overlooked both the heated pool and the steaming Jacuzzi. Beyond that, beyond the pond with bridges that separated the two, there were lighted tennis courts where Palmwood residents could play whenever they chose to. There was even a freebie ice dispenser where residents could freshen their drinks or, in case of a party, stock their freezers for guests.

"Palmwood welcomes you." Wanda stood in the center of the large, furnished living room. She tried to smile sincerely, but her eyes fell away when Lenny turned from the balcony to face her. She was a typical white woman . . . intimidated by the presence of "Negroes," and probably wondering if what people said about the length of a black man's penis was indeed true.

" 'Preciate you trouble," Lenny said. He stepped in off the balcony, looked from the electric fireplace to the leather swivel chair and foot stool, and from there to the plaid sofa that separated the living room area from the kitchen. There was a bedroom off to each side of that, one with just a shower, sink and commode, the other boasting a tub as well. It was indeed luxury living, and as white folks-oriented as the belly of a catfish. "Should o' bought us a bottle of champagne," he added, "an' invited y'all to a taste."

Wanda turned quickly to the door. Her face remained flushed. The eyes behind the rimless glasses flashed. "If . . . if you have any questions about our facilities, don't hesitate to stop at the clubhouse and ask," she said tersely.

"That mean you leavin'?" Jason said. He put his suitcase down, stood with hands on hips and studied the proper white lady.

"I . . . I have other duties," Wanda replied.

"Too bad," Jason added.

Lenny grinned. He, too, set his bag down, stood with hands on hips and studied the austere white woman. "Y'all invited to the house warmin'," he said. "Soon's we get our shit together, that is. Soon's we make the acquaintances o' all you fine, upstandin' tenants here 'bouts."

Wanda coughed. "W-welcome t-to Palmwood," she reiterated, and stepped quickly into the outer hall, closing the door to M-209 behind her.

Jason slapped his thigh, bent double with loud laughter. There were tears in his eyes when he looked up. "That proper white lady sure 'nough ain't ready fo' you, bro."

Lenny studied the closed door speculatively. He doubted whether anyone in Palmwood Gardens was ready for two black men from New York City. He doubted if California had counted on them. "Best get you shit unpacked," he told Jason. "Y'all got the bedroom with the shower. Me . . .?" He looked back over his shoulder at the wide balcony. He could hear the voices of white girls playing volley ball at the sand court near the steaming Jacuzzi. He had heard of Jacuzzis, but never had he experienced one. It was a new day all around, the Big Apple far behind: no fuzz to worry about, no more hassles. From now on, it was just him and Jason and partying until their money ran out. And after that . . . .

"Who care after that!" Lenny muttered.

"What that, bro?" Jason countered.

Lenny turned back to his friend, grinned. "Say as how you best get out o' you cutoffs," he said. "Say as how they a whole mess o' curious white gals downstairs, all just a-waitin' to eyeball us uppity niggas."

"Right on!" Jason said. He clutched at his nature, rolled his eyes.

"Then get you black behin' hoppin', mah man." Lenny crouched, jabbed playfully at his friend. "Heard tales 'bout what go down to that Jacuzzi at night. Best get us into some California courtin' clothes, go buy us a bottle at that shopping center 'round the corner an' see if them tales be true."

"Hey, bro," Jason said.

"Say on!"

"Don't go fallin' in love with one o' these blonde California mamas," Jason jived. " 'Specially that white office lady. That be like goin' from one jive humbolt to another."

"Shit!" Lenny said.

Jason winked, picked up his suitcase and disappeared into the bathtubless bedroom. Lenny frowned, turned back to the wide balcony and stepped outside to stare down at the pool and Jacuzzi. Palmwood was indeed a fine place, he mused. But the white folks were the same here—perhaps a little less straightforward—as back East. He and Jason were black . . . Jason almost charcoal. And they had stumbled upon whitey's haven, catching Wanda and the others off guard when they produced the rent money and fees. Now they were established for at least a month in the luxury apartment complex, perhaps the only *soul* in the entire place. The thought was at once spooky and ideal.

"Hey, main man," Jason called from the bedroom.

"Say on," Lenny reiterated.

"What you think them white gals gone do when they see this?" Jason appeared at the bedroom door. He was wearing his dungaree cutoffs, and pointing to the thing visible below one short pants leg.

It was Lenny's turn to bend double with loud laughter. Jason, the tip of his cock protruding below the cutoffs, was the stereotype black stud—hung heavy and bold! He could almost see the white girls at pool side ogling his friend's hefty, anxious nature. Already he could anticipate what would go down. "Just leave it hang where it be," he told Jason. "Y'all be puttin' it to good use 'fore midnight, if what I heard 'bout these luxury 'partment complexes be real."

"Hardship sure 'nough make me sad," Jason cried, picking up on what Lenny had said when they first arrived outside Palmwood Gardens.

CHAPTER TWO

IT TOOK LESS THAN AN HOUR to get their bags unpacked, clothes stored in the large sliding door closets in each bedroom, toothbrushes and razors and after-shave arranged on the wide, vanity-type counters with round sink and enormous mirror behind. Palmwood apartments were indeed plush, Lenny mused, his gaze moving approvingly from the vanity area to the comfortable, king-size bed, dresser, night table and pottery-base lamp. He wiggled his toes in the shag, wall-to-wall carpeting, grinned. "Hey, Jason," he called.

"Who that who say 'who that?' " Jason appeared in the open door to the bedroom across the living room. He had changed into dungaree cutoffs and sandals.

" 'Pears you all settled in." Lenny eyed his friend approvingly. Jason had always possessed a knack for fitting in. "Best we go find that shoppin' center 'round the corner, get us some food an' such," he added. "Get this place stocked with vitals 'fore we stock it with ho's."

Jason grinned. "Seen you an' that white lady lookin' each other up an' down."

"Shit!" Lenny scowled.

"Bet she do if you sock it to her," Jason countered. "Sure 'nough look like a frustrated bitch to me. Bet she shit an' fart an' pee the bed if y'all get what you after."

Stepping into his clogs and reaching for a shirt, Lenny moved into the living room. He eyed the kitchen area. Jason was right, he silently admitted. There was something about the white lady, a subdued sexiness, that made him want her. She reminded him of the sedate white social worker who used to visit his mother back in the city when he was still a boy. He tried to recall that one's name, couldn't. But he remembered the afternoon she arrived to find his mother out shopping, him alone in the four-room Harlem apartment, and how she eyeballed the fly of his boxer shorts for half an hour before he, only 16 then, mustered the courage to move to the worn and lopsided sofa and sit beside her. And then the move of his hand to her knee, and slowly upward while the nervous honkie talked at him about the Welfare Department's responsibility toward youngsters like him.

"I . . . I want to help you in . . . in *any* way I can," the white social worker had said.

"Sound fine." His 16-year-old hand had reached her full thigh, fingers inching close to the legband of her panties. He watched her close her eyes, tremble.

"M-my job demands that I g-get to know all my case people on a . . . on a *personal* b-basis," she croaked.

That sounded fine, too, Lenny recalled now. He remembered the look on the social worker's face—almost pain—when his fingers slipped beneath the panties and cupped at her wet pussy. He remembered the small moan when his stink finger pushed in, and how pretty she was when the rimless glasses came off, and her hair, pinned close to her head, fell in black-brown cascades over the worn cushions of his mother's sofa. He could envision Wanda like that . . . the skirt of the austere business suit bunched high on her waist, white thighs spread and pussy open for the stabs of his cock. Black meat: every woman he'd ever known was crazy for *that* kind of *personal basis* with brothers.

"Hey, bro, where you at?" Jason prompted.

Lenny laughed. He looked from his friend back to the barren kitchen. "Thinkin' 'bout a social case worker used to bring mah maw pots an' pans an' jive fo' the house back in Harlem," he said. "Ever' month after I was 16 . . . always on shoppin' day."

Jason frowned. "Never heard o' no case worker back to the city doin' that."

"Lots o' things that white lady done ain't nobody never heard of." Lenny stared again about the kitchen, mentally cataloguing the items they needed to make the place go. He forgot about the white social worker, thought instead of the priorities of the moment—food and utensils—and what the Jacuzzi downstairs would be like after dark. He wondered if all the things he'd heard about Southern Californians being "swingers" were true. He moved to the door, motioned Jason to follow. He locked the apartment and moved pensively down the lighted hall and wondered if Wanda, the witch from the lobby who had the potential of being a *bona fide* fox, lived at the complex. And, if she did, if she'd have the nerve to confront him in a bathing suit.

"For a man just got to California, you sure spendin' lots o' time someplace else," Jason commented.

Again Lenny brought himself back to the business at hand. "Got lots o' time to spend in California," he said. "Right now . . . ."

Lenny crouched, jabbed playfully at his friend.

"Right now, y'all just a nigger come home to that white lady's jive paradise," Jason supplied.

The shopping center was within walking distance of the apartment complex and boasted everything from a combination super market-liquor store to separate men's and women's haberdasheries and a head shop. There were even carts supplied by the shopping center for patrons who lived at Palmwood, the carts collected at the complex each morning by youngsters who made their spending money through the pickup and delivery service. But Lenny and Jason knew none of this. All they were aware of was the fact that they had spent a small fortune stocking two of the carts, and now, once again at the door to their two bedroom, tired and hot, there were bags to be carried inside, food and booze and cigarettes to store before they partook of the luxurious Palmwood facilities.

"Got us more 'n enough to last out the month," Jason commented between trips from the cart to the kitchen.

"That's the idea, dude," Lenny told him. "Don't wanna do nothin' 'cept relax in the sun in the day, shoot down some pool balls an' some women at night."

Jason stood with hands on hips at the side of the bar-like kitchen counter. "Then what you jivin' fo'?" he demanded. "Near dark now, an' that pool an' Jacuzzi sure looked well-stocked when we come up here."

Lenny grinned and stroked himself obscenely. "Must've know'd some black cock on it's way to the coast, bro. Those ladies just down there like some kind of greetin' committee!"

Jason laughed, turned to the refrigerator and pulled

19

out a six pack of Bud. "C'mon, let's see if all those jive stories true!"

The sky to the west had turned a bright orange as sunset slowly turned into dusk. Polynesian torches burned brightly around the pool and the Jacuzzi, giving the central courtyard an exotic, if not dreamlike, flavor. A few people swam in the crystal waters of the pool, but the bodies which had been plastered around its edges earlier in the day had disappeared.

"Can't abide by the situation here," Lenny commented as he stood above the huge pool and stared into the water. "Them foxes got their white bitch tans and split!"

"Yeah," Jason nodded, turning his gaze beyond the wooden bridge and to the huge Jacuzzi on the other side. "Looks like they opted for some mellow times in that Jacuzzi."

The Jacuzzi, being at least thirty feet in length and ten feet across, could accommodate an incredible number of people. The roar of the hot water jets drowned out the sound of voices, and all that was perceived were the silent forms of white, bikini-draped bodies sitting quietly amidst the turmoil.

Lenny and Jason stood at the edge of the pleasure pond and stared down at the blonde nymphs relaxing in the swirling waters.

"A nigger's vision of heaven!" Lenny chuckled softly to his partner.

The blue eyes slowly turned upward to the two handsome black men as they stood at the edge of the Jacuzzi and surveyed the flesh below them. One girl, a striking blonde with a wicked Southern California tan, smiled directly at Jason. Her eyes moved down from his face, across his chest and rested finally on his groin. Jason shifted his weight and felt his sex stir.

"Looks like you just got your brain married," Lenny laughed.

Jason grinned. "Other parts, too . . . ."

"C'mon, bro, let's get our black asses into this thing!" Lenny lowered himself slowly into the hot water. He grinned broadly at the girls who continued to stare at him. Far across the Jacuzzi, sitting alone, was a big blond kid with a Buster Brown hairdo. He wasn't smiling, and his cold blue eyes were leveled directly at Lenny. As he submerged himself into the swirling water, Lenny managed to grin wickedly at the chiseled vision of Orange County white supremacy.

"He lame or stoned?" Jason grinned as he sat on the step next to Lenny.

"Most likely a little of both, Jason. Man definitely a whitey, though, no doubt about that!"

The blonde nymph continued to stare at Jason, and he managed to catch a glimpse of her full, tanned thighs beneath the clear, swirling water. He could see that she was shifting herself, moving her legs slowly back and forth against one another. Jason reached behind him and tore off two beers, extending one in the direction of the little blonde.

"Hey, groovey," she smiled as she reached out and took the cool can of Bud. "Thanks."

"Hey, baby, that's cool. We got 'bout everythin' to make times happy."

The girl stood up in the shallow water, letting both Jason and Lenny glimpse her full, ripened white flesh. She wore a pink translucent bikini which left little to the imagination. Her full breasts were outlined beneath the bra, and her large, pointed nipples peeked out seductively. Her firm belly gave way to the top edge of her panties, and below that the triangular outline of her pussy was completely visible. Jason took a deep breath and a large swig on his beer.

"My name's Debbie," she said, standing above the two black men with the water pulsating around her upper thighs. "You dudes live here?"

"We just made it in," Jason replied. "Figured we'd check some of that famous California action."

Debbie smiled, her eyes moving back and forth from Jason to Lenny. "I think you'll find it pretty hip, if you know what I mean."

"Already have, mama, already have." Jason patted the seat next to him and Debbie sprung to his side. He could feel the warmth of her flesh as she pushed her leg directly against his.

"You live 'round here, baby?" Jason asked.

Debbie shook her head. "Not exactly. I mean, I'm sort of hung up at home right now. But I hope to get my own place soon as I get a job."

"Hey, that's cool. You just come here to party, then?"

"Yeah, my home's a real bummer. My parents don't understand anything . . . specially about drugs, or having a good time. They don't know what life is all about."

Jason grinned broadly. "An' I can tell by the way you move that you does, little mama."

Lenny nudged Jason kiddingly, then moved off the stoop and half floated, half walked across the length of the Jacuzzi. He thought about his partner, and the fact that two minutes into their new lifestyle the man had already scored. It had always been that way with Jason. Back in New York the man just had to walk into a bar and he was getting action. Lenny laughed to himself, thinking it always took him at least five minutes longer.

He was still chuckling softly to himself when he came face to face with the blond kid sitting at the far end. For a brief moment, Lenny tensed, clenching his fists beneath the water and preparing for some kind of action. The blond just sat at the edge of the pool and stared at him.

"How's it going, man?" he said finally.

Lenny nodded. "Cool," he replied softly.

"Yeah, I can dig it."

The kid spoke with slurred speech, trying to subdue his tone so that his voice sounded deeper. Lenny almost laughed when he talked. He had heard hundreds of white kids talking this way before, an induced speech pattern directly resulting from ingestion of downers. And even when they were straight, they spoke in the same patterns. Always slow, always hip. To Lenny, they had become the lames—the big, long-haired loons with funny looking haircuts and vacant eyes. They were laughable, but they were also dangerous. Like large men who possessed the emotional make-up of children, they walked through life never fully understanding their own physical power. You had to watch yourself around them. They were a new breed, and all the analysis had yet to come in on them.

"Some nice action around here," the big blond said, still not smiling, but staring at Lenny with those cold, washed out blue eyes.

"It's different than the big town, my man," Lenny smiled, running on a little of the southern comfort drawl.

"You from New York, huh?"

"That's right, brother. The big time Apple. Now, there's a place that got you some action. An' I can see you're a man who appreciates all the action he can get!"

For the first time the blond smiled. His teeth, white and even, shone beneath the glazed flesh of his summer tan. "My name's Don, man," he said, extending his hand.

Lenny took his hand, allowing Don to take him through his own version of the triple handshake. When they had finished, Don slapped Lenny's opened palm, then giggled.

"You turn on?" Don asked.

"Damned straight, soul brother." Lenny grinned. "You know all us brothers like the hemp now and then. 'Course, we like other kinds of action, too."

Don nodded knowingly. "Yeah, I can dig it."

Lenny allowed the silence to remain for a second or two. He had dealt enough drugs to know when a lame was coming on to him. Obviously, he laughed to himself, a black man here in Palmwood Gardens would have drugs, stuff to keep these soft-headed little rich kids stoned and happy. Make them all feel hip, like they were real men having real experiences of life. Lenny had always insisted that if he and Jason could have somehow cornered one whitey suburban area for their drug market, they would be able to retire within a year. The white man's kids loved the stuff.

Don lit a cigarette and watched Lenny closely. Lenny knew he was waiting, but was enjoying the pause. At the far end of the Jacuzzi, Jason was sipping beer with the beautiful Debbie, while another girl, a brunette, had edged up to his other side. Lenny smiled. He knew his partner would be watching out for him, making sure that a little of that white pussy would come his way. He turned back to Don.

"My man," he began very slowly, "I don't mean to presume anything, until all the facts are justified, if you can dig where I'm coming from."

Don nodded. "I can dig it."

"But, uh, it appears to my obvious sensibilities that you being a dude living in the realm of the cool, might just be interested in doing a little business. Am I rolling in oregano or speaking it plain?"

Don smiled. "Well, man, I think you're right on."

"That's cool. That's very cool. Now, we can get down to the basics. What can I do for you?"

Don hesitated a moment before answering. "Quaaludes?" he whispered finally.

Lenny took one of Don's cigarettes and lit it, exhaling slowly and with meaning. He was playing him by ear. He had no idea what the traffic was like out here on the West Coast, had no idea what the white kiddies in Orange County were getting and for how much. He had to insert a little drama into the scene to make it work.

"Well, my man," Lenny breathed, "what you talkin' here is some mighty powerful medicine. I mean, the dudes on the streets back in Harlem, well, they play real hard for that real shit like the 'ludes. You dig?"

Don was impressed. The big guy had spent his years walking the quiet streets of Orange County and thinking about little more than the upcoming game in which he held forth on the front line. He had seen very few blacks, most of his exposure had come from television and the movies. Insulated would have been a good word to use for him except for the fact that he assumed much and knew very little.

"So what are they going down for?" Don asked after a long silence.

Lenny shrugged his shoulders, silently damning the Hollywood film people who gave "niggers" jive dialogue and taught the little white boys how to speak like them. "Guess you could say two a pop."

Lenny watched Don, sizing up his reaction.

"I don't know, man, that's pretty steep."

Lenny chuckled. "Shit man, you talkin' west coast junk, produced in Mexico, know where I'm coming from? Dudes back home, they use only the *primo* source material. I guess you just get what you pay for."

Lenny turned and started wading back to the other side of the Jacuzzi. Don called out after him. "Hey man, hold on a second . . . ."

Upstairs, in his apartment, Lenny poured Don a Jack Daniels on the rocks and sat down at the dining room table to count out a hundred of the tranquilizers. Don sat across from him, fingering the hundred dollar bills in his hand, sipping almost effeminately on the drink.

"The chicks really get off on this stuff here 'bouts, eh?" Lenny mumbled as he counted the pills.

"You can lay any broad in the complex with a quaalude. Lay them twice if you got some coke."

Lenny glanced sharply at Don. "Coke, eh? You guys big into coke?"

Don grinned. "Yeah."

"Rich man's drug," Lenny said slowly. "Rich man's drug."

Don slid the money across the table toward Lenny. "Some of us can manage it."

"Guess so, brother. Guess so."

After Don left with his pills, Lenny poured himself a drink and moved out onto the balcony. He smiled as he watched the huge, lumbering figure cross the courtyard toward the Jacuzzi. Don leaned down over one of the girls, whispered something in her ear, and stood up. She jumped like a trained dog out of the heated waters and followed him into the hallway across from the pool. Lenny chuckled quietly. His profit on that five minute "lame trade" had been nearly eighty percent. Another quick mark like the blond football hero and he and Jason would have the rent paid for yet another month.

In the Jacuzzi below, Jason sat between Debbie and her friend, talking and gesturing up toward the balcony wher Lenny stood. Dumb as he was, Don had taught him something about the style of making it in Palmwood Gardens. And it appeared that Jason was having some trouble getting the girls upstairs. Lenny swigged down the remainder of his drink and headed back down to the Jacuzzi.

"Hey brother, what's happenin'?" Lenny called out as he knelt behind the trio. Both girls turned and looked at him, their eyes once again traveling to his groin.

"Leonard, my man, like you to meet two fine ladies. This here's Debbie and Kris. They come every once in a while lookin' for a party."

"Well, ladies, you come to the right place. Me and Jason here got so hot throwin' down some big ones in the Big Apple the mayor had to ask us to leave. No one was showing up for work no more."

The two girls giggled, and the fine jiggling of Kris' large breasts did not escape Lenny's gaze.

Lenny had learned his lesson well, and the mention of quaaludes prompted the two girls out of the pool and up the stairs to the black men's apartment. They both stood side by side just inside the front door, suffering from a temporary apprehension. Their golden flesh still dripped with water, their skimpy bikinis barely covered their still budding bodies.

"Now you ladies just relax," Jason began quickly, running to the kitchen and pulling out a bottle of Tanqeray gin. "Me and Lenny goin' demonstrate how guests are treated in New York."

Lenny took Kris by the hand and led her to the sofa. She sat down demurely, closing her thighs tightly together. But her eyes were victims of her own curiosity, unable to keep from gazing at the bulge in Lenny's cut-offs. Lenny noticed this, and grinned.

"Listen, Kris," he began sincerely, "you look uncomfortable in that wet suit. How about a nice towel to wrap around your fine body?"

Kris looked quickly to Debbie, almost as though seeking approval. Debbie just smiled, showing a perfect set of white teeth. "Okay," Kris said finally.

Lenny took her by the hand and led her to his side of the apartment. He closed the door which led to the bedroom and bathroom behind him. He leaned down over the young white girl and kissed her boldly, his tongue immediately worming its way deep inside her mouth.

Kris turned instantly. Her hand went down to the huge bulge and she began stroking him. She sighed when she realized how big it was.

Lenny touched her white flesh as though it were a fine piece of ivory. His hands roamed softly across her shoulders, down between her full breasts and to her belly. When his fingers played at the elastic of her bikini panties, Kris began squirming, trying to move herself farther away.

"Uptight, little mama?" Lenny asked softly.

"No, it's not that," Kris said simply. "It's just that . . . well, I've got someone here."

Lenny backed off and feigned surprise. "Well now, hard to believe fine young thing like yourself wouldn't have nobody. It don't bother me."

Kris turned away for a moment, straightening her bra which had become unhinged. "That guy you left the pool with? He's my boyfriend's roommate."

"Shit, mama! Can't have everything."

Kris turned her wide blues upward and looked directly into Lenny's face. "But you're different . . . I mean, your people, they've always been mistreated, hated by white people. If Jimmy found out."

Lenny turned quickly away and lit a cigarette. Memories of the social worker in New York flooded his mind. The same kind of condescending bullshit, the same weeping pity which white women horny for black cock have always used as a rationale for spreading their thighs and taking that "gorilla" meat inside their tight little pussies. And now, coming from a little white girl, a girl with straight white teeth, it was a little much. It seemed that the latest educational progress was in the area of pity, pitying the inferior.

"Listen," Kris began earnestly, "I don't have anything against you. I was just trying to warn you, that's all."

Lenny turned back to face her. His cock was ruling the moment, the political outrage could wait for another time. Her little white body was much too inviting to begin a discourse on human relations. "I know how you feel, honey," he began in his most sincere voice. "We been living with that fear for three hundred years. But from generation to generation, they done passed down the strength, the will to survive. We just waiting for the white man to understand, is all."

Kris looked up into Lenny's face with worshipful eyes. Without speaking, she began untying the string which secured her bra. Slowly, she pulled the cups away from her breasts. They were pearl white, rounded, with perfectly formed nipples capping each cone with a delicious pink.

"You do understand," Lenny mumbled as he ran his tongue across his lips, anticipating the white sundae in store for him.

"I do, I do . . ." Kris whispered. She hooked her thumbs into the elastic of her panties and shimmied the skimpy garment down across her hips. As the material slid down her thighs, Lenny stared at the patch of dark pubic hair, light and sparse which surrounded her soft, pink lips.

She was not like a black woman at all, Lenny thought to himself. The pubic hair was feathery, almost non-existent. The coarse texture which he had found on so many sisters was gone. And the lips themselves, pink like a little white girl's. Almost virginal.

Kris stepped out of her panties and stood naked in front of the black man. "Now you," she said hoarsely. She reached out and snapped open the button to his cut-offs, then struggled with the zipper as she tried to bring it down across his swollen sex. When she had finally accomplished this, she dropped to her knees and pulled the Levis the rest of the way down.

Lenny stood above her, his hands resting gently on her still moist hair. He felt her lip's feathery touch as she gently kissed the underside of his cock. Then her tongue, tracing the length slowly until she reached the tip. Her mouth opened wide to accommodate him, and she sucked him inside gently.

"Am I all you thought I'd be?" Lenny asked.

Kris nodded, and groaned. Her white mouth was full of him, and she could not speak.

"I thought so," Lenny said as he thrust himself deeper into her lily white throat.

Jason drained the Jack Daniels from his glass and walked slowly to the kitchen for a refill. Debbie watched him with vacant, watery eyes. The quaaludes had begun taking effect and, combined with the liquor, were slowing her down to a snail's pace. But she was happy, and Jason could see, ready to roll.

"So me an' my partner, Lenny, decided to split the coast and come to land of milk and honey. 'Course," Jason began, smiling at the beautiful blonde sitting on the couch, "we didn't dream it'd be in human form."

Debbie giggled, took a large swig of her drink and placed the glass on the coffee table. She got to her feet, struggling a little as her light-headed state made it difficult for her to move, and ambled out onto the balcony. Jason followed her closely.

Below them, the Jacuzzi was still filled with people. A couple of the girls were sitting nude beneath the swirling waters, talking quietly amongst themselves while a group of men sat at the other end. Jason chuckled softly.

"What's funny?" Debbie asked.

"Man, those jive turkeys down there, that's what funny! Couple fine ladies don't even bother to wear no bathing suits, and them fools stick it out at the other end! Be embarrassed to call myself a man."

It was Debbie's turn to laugh. "That's just it. They're fags. Lot of fags living in this place. It's kinda nice sometimes. A girl doesn't feel uptight, you know?"

"Oh lord! Fag heaven. Jesus Christ, you people got a little bit of everything goin' down here, ain't ya?"

Debbie staggered against the railing and nodded. Jason put his arm on her shoulder to steady her, then allowed his hand to slide down bare skin until his fingers rested on the soft flesh of her breast. "I'm glad you're not that way, Jason," Debbie mumbled.

"Ain't no such thing as a black fag, pretty mama. Niggers' too ugly to be fags."

Debbie giggled and turned herself toward Jason, letting his hand slide beneath the material of her bra and cup her breast. Her nipple hardened immediately and she moaned softly.

Jason could feel her body sag, and any tension which had been present before subside. He had felt the same thing with the women of New York, the sisters who hungered madly after the soothing rush of the white powder, shooting it anywhere including their pussies. They had all been tough, and their flesh had shown the effects of years in the ghetto. The white girl he held now in his arms was flawless. Her skin was unblemished, her body still firm and taut. She possessed the smooth lines of the young, and streets had not eaten her up alive.

"C'mon mama," Jason said tenderly, "let's get us into bed."

Debbie reached down and grasped the bulk of his sex and squeezed it gently. She gasped at the size, then began giggling.

"Tol' you we ain't faggity. Too damned ugly."

"You're beautiful!" Debbie laughed, still holding him down there as he led her into his bedroom.

CHAPTER THREE

IT WAS THREE-THIRTY IN THE MORNING when Debbie and Kris finally left the apartment. Still living with their parents in nearby Newport Beach, they were not allowed to stay out all night. Three-thirty was bad enough, and as they staggered from the apartment, still wearing their bathing suits, they looked more like frightened children than women who had been sexually satiated for more than three hours of non-stop erotic play.

"Fine little bodied foxes," Lenny chuckled after closing the door behind them.

"Man, them ladies just want the feel of nigger cock and they'll do anything to get a taste."

Lenny playfully punched at Jason. "An' I'll bet that fine little all-American blonde got herself one taste after another!"

"I didn't see you sitting out here watching the tube with yours, my man!" Jason swung back, gently slapping Lenny's face.

"Goddam, nigger, we got ourselves a made situation around this jive lame joint." Lenny sat down and lit a cigarette. "Know that blond moron from the Jacuzzi earlier this evenin'?"

Jason nodded. "Kid who looked like something out a science fiction movie, like some kinda robot or somethin'?"

"Yeah, that was the dude. Come up here an' lay two bills on me for a hundred quaaludes. Tol' me every piece in this white heaven goes down real easy under the influence. Tol' me they go down twice as fast with cocaine, man." Lenny took a long drag on his cigarette and smiled to himself. "Yes sir, brother, we not only got ourselves a pussy machine happenin' up here, but we got a genuine, honest to goodness income! All them whiteys think dope from the hands of a nigger twice as good as anything they get at the high school. Goddamn!"

Jason mixed a drink for each of them. "We just a couple of hip, mean dudes, man. This is like walking into a goddamn candy store and takin' any piece we choose."

Lenny raised his drink in a toast. "To the dark dudes of Palmwood Gardens, man. May the place rattle and roll beneath our touch!"

They laughed as they sipped their drinks. When they

had finished, Jason suggested one more round with the Jacuzzi before turning in. "Seems like the place never shuts down, brother, and best we take advantage of it."

And, indeed, it never did shut down. The Jacuzzi was going full blast when the pair arrived. In the darkened corner, a woman, wearing a string bikini which showed off a dark, almost wrinkled tan, smiled up at them as they approached. She appeared to be one of those middle-aged females who spend much too much time in the sun, turning their flesh to a consistency similar to leather. But she was still not bad looking, even with her bleached hair. In her youth, she could have been a real looker. Now, she was just hanging on to what little she had left, making the most of an ageing situation.

Sitting next to her was a young man, barely twenty, with long hair and an attempt at a mustache. He was skinny and emaciated, looking as though he had been on speed for a long time. His skin was pale, and the muscled body so common amongst the Southern California surfer was not evident. The woman seemed to dominate him, and when Lenny and Jason approached the Jacuzzi, it was obvious that she had her hand on his groin. She did not remove it as the two black men slid into the water across from her.

"Hi there," she said brightly.

Both Jason and Lenny grinned.

"My name's Sylvia. You boys new here?"

"Yeah, we're new." Lenny said quickly, his voice cold. The term "boys" hadn't sat too well. Had he known, he would have realized that Sylvia referred to anyone younger than herself, which was practically everybody, as "boy."

Sylvia continued to regard both Jason and Lenny with interest. She moved up on the step, allowing her full breasts exposure and even going so far as to adjust her bra so that more of her cleavage was visible. "My name's Sylvia, and this is Clark."

Clark nodded sleepily to both men. He was obviously stoned out of his mind. His eyes did not focus, his drawn face did not register anything.

"My boy and I here love to take Jacuzzis," Sylvia began again, brightly, "especially late at night. No one's around then, and it gives us a chance for a little *au naturel* bathing."

"You mean skinny dipping?" Jason blurted.

Sylvia laughed. "Very funny! Of course I do. The Jacuzzi should always be taken without a suit. It ruins the effect if you have to wear clothing."

Jason and Lenny looked at each and grinned. The place was too much. Even when the old ladies came out, they had nothing but sex on their minds.

"Would you boys mind?" Sylvia began, standing so that the full length of her body was out of the water. She did not wait for their response, but instead stripped off her top and just as quickly pulled down her panties. She threw the wet suit on the coping, then turned slowly toward Jason and Lenny. "Clark?" she said firmly, still staring at the two blacks across from her.

Clark struggled with his suit, and finally pulled it off. It didn't seem to matter to him, it was obvious he had no idea where he was.

"If you boys care to join me . . ." Sylvia said, touching her breast lightly.

Lenny looked at Jason, and Jason at Lenny. "Why not?" they said in unison.

Sylvia watched eagerly as both men stood and yanked off their cut-offs. Their black manhood sprung to life, and the old woman smiled. "See, doesn't that feel a whole lot better?" she asked.

"Sure does, ma'am," Lenny said in a slurred voice as

he sat back into the water. "Makes people look prettier, too," he added.

Sylvia smiled. "I think so, too."

No one noticed the looming, overweight figure dressed in uniform and carrying an eight cell flashlight which doubled as a nightstick standing above them. Thadius "Thad" Jones would wait it out. It was his duty to rid the Jacuzzi of the nudies in the wee hours of his long shift, but sometimes it was interesting to stand around a little and take in the sight. For his peon's salary of one fifty per week, the forty-five-year-old black man felt what ever kicks he could wrangle from the complex were rightfully his.

"Okay," Thad drawled finally, "back on with the suits."

Sylvia moaned loudly. "Oh God, not you again!"

"That's right, ma'am. You know it ain't by the rules to go on swimmin' without a bathing suit."

"How boring! C'mon Clark, let's go upstairs where we can be ourselves a little!" Without putting her suit on, and with only a towel draped loosely over her shoulders, the older woman grabbed her young friend by the hand and led him from the Jacuzzi. She turned to Jason and Lenny and smiled. "See you two soon, I hope."

Both Jason and Lenny nodded, then watched the ageing body and the young, skinny kid as they made their way into the apartment building across from the Jacuzzi.

Thadius stood above the two with his hands on his hips and a big grin spread across his face. "Showin' off your black legends?" he kidded easily.

Lenny grinned. "The name's Lenny, brother. And this here's Jason. We just got in from New York."

Thadius knelt down and shook both men's hands.

"You got to realize I was the only nigger hereabouts, and too old to do anything about it. Leastways now I can dig on your action."

"Right on," Lenny chuckled. "You been holdin' out here long?"

"Ever since the damned place opened. Seven years ago. Makin' myself ten dollars a week more now. Got to deal with white hopheads and spoiled little rich kids day in and day out. Glad to see a couple of brothers finally makin' it by."

"Shit," Jason began, "we just here for a little while, digging on some kind of nigger dream, if you dig where I'm comin' from."

Thadius nodded. "I was thirty-eight when I took this gig, figured I'd have two, maybe three good years making some of this white ass always walking around half-naked. Got pretty good for a while, but I got too old for that kind of shit. And too tired of white boy's mind."

"I can dig that wholly!" Lenny agreed. "Seem like there's nothing but lames 'round here. I mean, this where whitey send his boys who ain't got no brains or what?"

This broke Thadius up, and he shook slightly as he regained his breath. "Man oh man, it's good to hear some kind of talk you layin' down, brother. I was beginnin' to feel like some kind of damned zoo keeper."

"Well listen here, Thadius," Jason began, "long as me and my partner holding down some action around here, things'll be lookin' up for us nigger souls."

"I can dig that!" Thadius grinned, slapping each man's hand energetically. "Now you dudes get on your suits, and I'll show you around. Lot goes on here at night nobody knows 'bout 'cept me. These white folks do have some kind of strange night life, no doubt."

The complex at night seemed even larger than it did during the daylight hours. Row upon row of three story building, wandering paths between them, little niches and corners locked away in dark places. The grounds were like a maze, and the traveler without a map could easily become lost.

Thadius, walking with a noticeable limp, ambled through the winding pathways of Palmwood Gardens, speaking softly to Lenny and Jason, who followed him.

"You got to remember," Thadius said as he turned into a courtyard ringed with apartments, "that this place started for one thing—sex. Ain't no way no one can't know that. So you get the young gals in here, the ones who want to play all the time. You get the young studs, too, white dudes who got nothin' but pussy on their minds and can afford to stay here."

Jason giggled. "Don' give 'em that much credit, Thadius. I ain't seen no evidence of no mind here yet!"

Thadius laughed softly, then continued. "An' then you saw yourself the middle-aged white woman, desperate as hell 'cause she ain' married yet. She'll stay here for years, man, just lookin' all the time. Some dude'll move in, and she'll move in real quick on him. But it don't never last with her, 'cause she's so desperate to get married she'll scare the guy off."

"What about that broad, Sylvia?" Lenny asked.

"She's got herself an inheritance or somethin'. Never works, just looks around for young meat. Don't think that woman can breathe les' she's got some hard cock inside her."

"Lame she was with tonight don't look he even got a cock no more."

"He been 'round for a couple of weeks. Looks like he on his way out." Thadius stopped short, and held out his hand to stop both Lenny and Jason. He pointed to a second story window, sitting behind a balcony. The drapes were drawn, and inside the well-lit room a young woman with long black hair was walking around smoking a cigarette. She was completely nude.

"Goes down like that here lots," Thadius commented. "Seem like white folks tryin' to get back to where we come from, the jungle. No one like wearing clothes."

The young woman paced the floor of her apartment, nervously smoking a cigarette. Her body was good, although her breasts were small. Lenny thought of how much she looked like a sister waiting for a hit, waiting for her man to return from the streets with a nickel bag. That same kind of ravaging tension was apparent.

"A bitch in heat," Jason mused, chuckling to himself as he stroked his groin.

Thadius grunted. "Know that lady. She calls me once, maybe twice a month and complains 'bout some stud tryin' to force his way in there. Bet she know we down here right now, gettin' all itchy just watchin' her."

"You mean she just gets off showin' off herself like that without ever doin' nothin' about it?"

"That's right, Lenny. Far as I know, ain't been no man here put it to her yet."

"Jesus shit," Lenny laughed. "White bitches something else!"

Thadius turned away from the window. "Show you some fun, if'n you're ready."

Jason and Lenny both nodded enthusiastically. They were enjoying themselves thoroughly. The old black security guard had obviously not spent his time here in oblivion. He had made a study of the place, and knew the characters who inhabited this concrete jungle of erotic tensions. The man, both Jason and Lenny decided was something of a genius in his own right.

Thadius led Lenny and Jason through what seemed like an endless maze of corridors, hallways and pathways until finally they emerged upon a small courtyard somewhere near the tennis courts. Surrounding the courtyard were two large apartment wings, with many of the windows opened and lights beaming softly into the night.

"Okay, just follow me," Thadius said almost gleefully. "We'll nail ourselves one white pigeon."

Thadius ducked behind some bushes, and Lenny and Jason followed suit. They waited, crouched in the early morning hours, for fifteen minutes. And then they heard it, footsteps moving with an uneven pace toward them. Every few seconds or so, the steps would stop, then a rustle of bushes, then the steps agin.

Finally, a tall, distinguished man with a mustache and stylishly long hair appeared directly in front of the waiting trio. The man wore a navy blue blazer, white yachting pants and deck shoes. He held a leash upon which scrambled a little, properly trimmed poodle.

"A former admiral in the Navy," Thadius whispered.

The admiral stood in the center of the courtyard looking about slowly. Finally, he spotted something which held his interest and began moving quietly and quickly in the direction of one of the first story windows. A soft red light shone from the window, and soon the admiral was crouched directly beneath it, his body partially hidden by the bushes.

Thadius stood slowly, joined by Lenny and Jason. They could see the silhouetted form of a woman moving about in the room behind the window. She appeared to be in the act of undressing.

The admiral stayed motionless beneath the window, peering in just over the sill. Thadius backed up the walk about a hundred feet, then began walking toward the old man. He accentuated his steps so that the admiral would be sure to hear him.

The scene beneath the window was comical. The old man turned immediately to his dog and began speaking softly to it, sounding as though he was coaxing her to relieve herself. Then, as he saw Thadius, he began speaking in a harsher voice. "Bad girl, running away from daddy like that! Bad girl!"

Lenny and Jason watched the show from behind the bushes, each afraid that he would burst out laughing and destroy everything.

"Having problems, Admiral Simmons?" Thadius asked easily as he limped toward the Navy man.

"Hello Thadius," the admiral whispered in a clipped, Eastern accent. "Lexington here decided she would test her survival ability out here in the jungle. Just took off. I've been searching high and low for her all evening.

Thadius scratched his head. "Seems like that animal of yours always breaking loose, Admiral. Best you get her some trainin'."

"That's an excellent notion Thadius," the admiral replied. "I shall enter it into my log for tomorrow's activities."

"Best you do that, Admiral. Best you do that."

The admiral reached down and picked up his little poodle, then adjusted his coat. He was visibly disturbed. "Well, time to turn in, Thadius. Good night."

" 'Night, Admiral." Thadius stood with hands on his hips and watched the admiral disappear into the cavernous depths of the complex.

Lenny and Jason crawled from their positions in the bushes and began laughing loudly. Old Thadius just grinned. "See what I mean 'bout white man being freaky?"

"Damn!" Lenny laughed. "He really an admiral?"

"So the story goes. 'Course, beginning of World War Two, everybody got to be a general or an admiral, just weren't enough bodies to go around. Nope, just weren't enough white bodies to go around."

Jason shook his head back and forth, emitting a soft chuckle. "He use that lame dog story every time?"

"Yup. Ain' no way, but he suspects I just one poor, lame-brained nigger can't remember from one night to the next. Figures it's easy to fool old Thadius, that's what he does."

"Well, Thadius," Lenny mused, "you just keep them thinking that. Us niggers're going to show these lames a thing or two. I mean, they call this dive Palmwood Gardens, but far as I'm concerned, it's still the jungle. An' me and my partner been surviving in the jungle long time. Far as I can see, these white children can't even make it from the bedroom to the bathroom without pissing all over themselves."

Thadius regarded Lenny seriously. "Sure would be nice if some of these folks look at old Thadius differently."

Lenny took the old man's hand and shook it. "Don't worry yourself about that, old man. Your day will come."

He was over six feet tall, weighed somewhere in the neighborhood of two hundred pounds, and was very white. He stood, leaning against Lenny and Jason's apartment door, arms folded across his chest. He smoked a cigarette, and when he saw Thadius with Lenny and Jason, threw the butt onto the carpeted floor and ground it out slowly with the toe of his boot.

"You Lenny, boy?" he asked with a belligerent tone to his voice.

Lenny moved past him and jammed his key into the lock. "That's my name, motherfucker."

The white boy grabbed Lenny by the shoulders and spun him around, throwing him against the far wall. Lenny felt his shoulders crack as he hit the wall, and slid slowly to the floor. "What the fuck?" he demanded, he was shocked and stupified that some white man would take him on with two other brothers, one of them a security guard, standing nearby.

"You fucked Kris tonight, didn't you?" the white man demanded.

Lenny eyed him carefully, shaking his head. Behind the white man, Thadius moved up closely. He had the huge flashlight poised and ready to strike.

"You goddamn niggers move in here and start fucking around with white girls! Goddamn, we're going to kill you!" The white man took a flying leap at Lenny, but he missed his mark. Lenny spun himself out of the way, and the white man plunged headfirst against the wall. The sound was sickening as his head crunched against the plaster.

Thadius came up quickly behind him, dropped his knee into the small of his back and used the flashlight as a billy club, bringing it hard up beneath the man's chin. "Now you listen, fucker," Thadius warned in a brutal, cold voice, "we don't tolerate none of this shit around here. You understand?"

The boy's senses began returning to him, the outrage he had been thriving on disappeared and was replaced by outright fear. The realization hit him that there were three black men standing over him, ready to beat the living shit out of him.

"Now, you go on home, boy," Thadius continued. "I don't want to see your kind making any more trouble around here. You dig?"

The kid nodded, his eyes bulging. He was awakening from a dream, and the fear was running rampant throughout his body. He began trembling, then a moist spot appeared at the crotch of his pants. Thadius climbed off him and grabbed an arm to get him to his feet. "Now get!" Thadius ordered. The white boy half ran, half stumbled down the hall and into the stairwell.

"You know that dude?" Thadius asked as he moved inside the apartment with Lenny and Jason.

"Shit man," Lenny complained, "his little white bitch picked me up at the Jacuzzi last night. Came up here and was so hot for black cock she couldn't be stopped."

Jason poured a round of Jack Daniels and passed them out. "Goddamn, Lenny, you been here one fucking day and you got half the complex on your ass. California ain't that godawful big!"

Lenny chuckled. "Man was crazy," he said softly. "Standing there with three niggers staring him down. Had to be crazy. Man on the streets would have run like shit. No way, these people all lame here, Jason. All lames."

Thadius drank his whiskey slowly, shaking his head back and forth. "You two the first black folks ever in this place," he began slowly, "and trouble already at hand. Company owns this joint, thing called Morris Properties, and they ain't going to like it none."

"He's right, Lenny," Jason added. "I mean, the lames here are one thing, the fucking corporation's another."

Lenny laughed. "Well, we already know enough about this place to get our own action going. Won't be too fucking hard to get a little of that white man's power for ourselves, if you can dig where I'm coming from."

45

Jason nodded. He had no idea what his partner was talking about. But he knew Lenny. And with him, there was always a method, always a way of taking adverse situations and bringing in the reins and taking control. The man never allowed the assholes to ride him.

"Hope you're right, nigger," Thadius said, raising his glass in a toast, " 'cause if you ain't, we got ourselves some problems."

Lenny returned the toast. "Don't worry yourself, ol' man. I'm right. Always have been . . . ."

CHAPTER FOUR

WANDA MORRISON did not live in Palmwood Gardens. She felt, upon accepting the job with Morris Properties, that it would have been highly unprofessional for her to reside at the place of her employment. And her career as a fast-rising woman executive with the huge corporation outstripped any other considerations she might have had. At the relatively young age of thirty-four, the bright divorcee was determined to reign as one of the first female executives in the corporation.

The small, tidy apartment which Wanda called home was situated in a quiet, remote sector of Newport Beach. Her neighbors were mostly retired executives; businessmen who had come to the expensive Southern California beach community to enjoy their golden years. It was perfect for Wanda, no hassles, and no men trying to push her into needless affairs. Her one boyfriend, a dull and rather unaccomplished lawyer, made her life as a woman seem respectable. Harold's main occupation with life certainly wasn't sex, and Wanda liked it that way.

As she dressed in front of the large maror, Wanda was careful to note her body. She stood naked, sucked in her belly and pulled back her shoulders. Her breasts were not very large, and had retained their firmness over the years. Her belly was flat and hard, and her hips flared nicely. Her auburn pubis was perfectly triangular, and meshed nicely with her well formed thighs. And when her hair was down, Wanda knew she could be a looker. It flowed richly across her shoulders, thick strands seductively covering her full nipples.

On the bed behind her lay her stiff tweed suit, her nylons and her black high-heeled shoes. Wanda turned slowly away from the mirror, saying goodbye to the image of a sexy woman and welcoming the suit of armor which she used for business. In the back of her mind lay the thought that someday she would be able to strip away the tweed and nylons and really let herself go. But before then, she would have to make her mark in business. There was no other way.

As she dressed, she thought about the young, brash black who had been so forceful with her the day before. In Newport Beach, her dealing with blacks had been almost non-existent. She had felt at once uncomfortable and excited by him, the danger which emanated from his coal black eyes had been unreal. Most of the men she had dealt with had been instantly intimidated by her mode of dress, and eventually wound up behaving like Harold—a bowl of pablum in a man's body. Not that she had wanted it any differently, of course. It was just that sometimes she did enjoy feeling like a woman. Even if it would never lead to anything, it was good for the old ego.

The morning routine at the Palmwood Gardens rental

offices was always the same. Coffee, maybe a plain donut, and talk with the girls for a few minutes. Of course, their conversations dealt mainly with members of the opposite sex and the preceding night's adventures. They had all learned long ago that when the subject of sex came up, their boss was to be tactfully excluded from the conversation.

"Any problems this morning?" Wanda asked Shirley, the first one in the morning.

Shirley grunted. "Those Negroes caused some kind of ruckus last night."

"Oh really?" Wanda said with raised eyebrows.

"It seems they got into a brawl in the hallway very early this morning."

"Was Thadius there?"

"Of course. He stopped it. But the neighbor who saw it said a nice-looking young man was just walking down the hall, minding his own business, when the two coloreds attacked him."

Wanda remembered the arrogant look in both black men's faces as they ambled through the apartment, the way they strutted and spoke down to everybody. At the time, she figured maybe there might be trouble. But she had not expected it so soon. "And what did Thadius say about this?" she asked Shirley.

Shirley laughed sardonically. "Take a guess. I mean, those people stick together, don't they? Thadius said the white boy jumped them for no apparent reason."

"It's possible," Wanda said, trying to sound light. "There are many people in this world who still cannot accept the Negro as part of humanity."

The point was missed entirely on Shirley. "I knew we should have turned them down yesterday. Nothing but trouble, everywhere the damned coons go!"

Wanda was shocked at Shirley's language. A gentile,

middle-aged lady whose greatest concern in life revolved around her Wednesday night domino games with the other older ladies of Palmwood Gardens, it was surprising to hear her talk like this.

"Now, Shirley," Wanda began slowly, as if speaking to a child, "you know if we had refused them, the NAACP might have investigated us. For all we know, the two colored gentlemen could be plants. They do that, you know."

"It figures," Shirley said, lighting a cigarette with a striking vengeance. "Those people ought to just stay where they are put. They're happier that way."

Wanda turned away from the plump old lady, disgusted with the tone of her voice and the expression of racism which came as a shock to her. She had never really had to deal with racial questions before, and there was nothing especially likeable about the two young blacks she had rented to the day before. But it was her job to keep Palmwood Gardens filled, and the men did have the money. It was business. And yet, after listening to Shirley's barrage, she was beginning to feel ashamed, and a little sorry for the two black men. If this was only the tip of the iceberg, then there was much more trouble down the line for everybody.

"To clear this up," Wanda said aloud so that everybody in the office could hear, "I'm going to speak with Thadius. He knows if he lies to me, his job is finished here."

"He'll lie," Shirley blurted.

"I'll have him sign a sworn affidavit. He knows the corporation will judge him on that."

Wanda picked up her purse and stormed from the office. She knew she had to quell the rumors as quickly as possible, to silent the quick and mean tongues of women like Shirley. Otherwise, there would be real trouble.

Thadius lived in nearby Santa Ana, in an old rundown house built over fifty years ago when the huge migration from the Midwest had settled Orange County. The families had come because of the land, and the farming opportunities available to them. For many years, Orange County had been one of the chief agricultural areas in California. But the times had changed, and the huge population expansion out of Los Angeles had pushed the farmers out to make room for housing tracts and mammoth apartment complexes like Palmwood Gardens.

Thadius opened the door, wearing a beat-up old bathrobe and looking very sleepy. His face registered shock at the sight of Wanda. He had never had the honor of a visit from anyone from Palmwood Gardens, even during the battle with influenza two years ago that almost took his life.

"I'm sorry to disturb you, Thadius," Wanda said, speaking slowly. "But it's very important that I speak with you."

"Sure thing, Miss Morrison." Thadius said, stepping aside and opening the door for her.

The tiny house was neat and clean. But it was a step twenty years backward in time. The sofa, chairs and table were musty and old. The walls were chipped and the wood trim rotting. The tiny icebox and stove looked like something out of a museum. Wanda Morrison had never seen a home like this. There aren't many in Newport Beach.

But Thadius would not comment on his surroundings. He played the host with class. "Won't you have a seat? Something to drink?"

"No thank you," Wanda said, taking a seat on the couch. The springs were broken, and a sharp pain riddled her buttocks. She grimaced, but would not move. "I'm here, Thadius, because of what happened last night outside apartment B-219."

Thadius nodded slowly. "Miss Shirley asked me about that this morning before I got off. I guess Mr. Turnbill across the hall saw the whole thing."

"The claim was that Lenny attacked the boy. Is that true?"

Thadius shook his head. "Uh uh, Miss Morrison. No way. That boy was standing outside Lenny's and Jason's apartment, waitin' on 'em. When Lenny got to the door, the boy jumped him, threw him clean across the hall and slammed him up against the wall. Lenny didn't even fight back, I had to stop the kid."

"But Shirley claims . . . ."

"She's lying, Miss Morrison," Thadius looked directly at Wanda, his eyes not wavering.

"I believe you, Thadius. But why? Why would some kid stand out there all night long waiting like that. And with two of them against just himself? It doesn't make any sense."

Thadius turned away, got up and went into the kitchen and poured himself a cup of coffee. He returned to find Wanda sitting on the edge of the sofa, eagerly awaiting an answer.

" 'Fraid I can't answer that, Miss Morrison."

"I think you know why, Thadius. And for their sake, as well as yours, you had better tell me."

Thadius shook his head, sipping slowly from the cup.

"Thadius," Wanda began imploringly, "I've got to have you sign a statement about what happened last night. Believe me, everyone's prepared not to believe. Unless, of course, there's a good reason for that kid to start a fight with Lenny."

"No one would believe it, anyway," Thadius

moaned.

"Try it. You've got to help me stop what's brewing at the Gardens before it gets out of hand."

"Okay, Miss Morrison. I'll tell you. But it might shock you."

"Try me," Wanda said with a smile.

"Well," Thadius began slowly, "this kid's name was Peter. He lives over in 'G' building with another guy named Don. Anyway, he's got a girlfriend, name Kris. Seem like Kris and Lenny spent the night together in Lenny's apartment. Peter found out. And that's why he was there waiting on them two boys."

"I see," Wanda said. A strange feeling erupted inside her at the thought of Lenny and a white girl spending time together, as she liked to put it when she and Harold had their bed dates. She found herself unable to speak for a moment, then envisioning the scene as it must have appeared in that bedroom. His black, glistening skin aginst hers, his cruel, cold mouth taking her down God knows what paths. It was an incredible vision for Wanda Morrison to have. Her mind had never dealt with sexual fantasy, she had always prevented it. But this time, the vision was too powerful for her to control.

"I'm sorry to have to tell you something like that, Miss Morrison. Being the kind of fine, upstanding woman that you are."

For a brief moment Wanda wanted to scream out, shock the hell out of the old Negro and tell him that she too does get naked with a man once in a while, does spread her legs and takes a man inside her. She almost laughed, however, when the moment passed and she saw in her mind's eye the flabby, pale body of Harold standing there, using his hand to excite himself as she lay naked on the bed. Thadius was right, but at least she had chosen the path herself, had made that determination a long time ago. It wasn't a problem, it was a choice.

Wanda Morrison drove back to Palmwood Gardens, carrying the signed statement by Thadius and a vision in her brain that would not let go. Black against white, flesh against flesh. It was completely disconcerting to the woman who had spent the better part of her twenties and early thirties establishing an image, a look that would fend off the weaknesses of the flesh in a world gone mad with pleasure. She had known long ago that to succeed it was necessary to overcome that madness first, and then progress as a superior being to the rest. But something was happening to her, and happening very quickly. It had been less than twenty-four hours since the two black men had moved into Palmwood Gardens, and already they had affected everyone there, including herself.

She stood in the hallway outside apartment B-219 and knocked lightly on the door. She felt jittery, and her palms were moist. She listened carefully to the movement on the other side of the door, and when she heard the latch being removed, she caught her breath.

Jason stood wrapped in a terrycloth bathrobe, smiling our at her. "Mornin' Miss Wanda," he said in his best Uncle Tom voice. " 'Fraid the cotton goin' to have to wait this mornin', Massuh, 'cause me and my pickin' friend done did some good partyin' last night."

"Oh, shut up with that bullshit and let me see Lenny!" The anger in her voice shocked her, as did the words which tumbled from her full lips.

Jason took a step backward and regarded with surprise. His mouth fell open, but suddenly he began laughing easily, and not without warmth. "You're kinda cute when you cuss," he chided.

Even Wanda had to smile. "I'm sorry, but it's important that I speak with Lenny."

"Get him roused right away. C'mon in and make yourself comfortable." Jason held the door open and watched her move into the living room. He could see now why Lenny had blown out behind the vision of her swaying hips. There was a lot of woman beneath those tweeds, Jason thought.

Lenny appeared moments later, a towel draped around his midsection. His lean, black body rippled as he moved, and his steps seemed to lift him off the floor. Wanda tried not to look at him as he crossed the floor toward the couch, but she felt her gaze drawn to the panther-like body.

"Mornin'," Lenny grinned, standing directly in front of her.

Wanda tried to smile, but her lips wer quivering so badly that they seemed permanently frozen. Her eyes were directed at his face, and directly in front of her was the large bulge beneath his towel. She felt her body tremble slightly, and the vision once again return.

"Get you some coffee, you look like you seen a ghost or something!" Lenny laughed as he moved to the kitchen and poured. Jason winked at his friend and returned to his bedroom.

"There are some questions to be answered, Lenny," Wanda began in a weak voice. "I just spoke with Thadius, and he said you were attacked."

"That's right," Lenny said easily, placing a cup of coffee in front of her. "Lousy motherfucker was waitin' on me. Lucky Thadius was around, could have gotten real bad."

Wanda took a sip of her coffee and almost choked as Lenny took a seat directly across from her. The towel he wore fell open, and his black cock was plainly in sight. It was obvious that Lenny was enjoying himself thoroughly.

"See, ma'am," Lenny began calmly, "sometimes, white folks, well, they think of us black folk as bein' just a little different. 'Specially the women, if you know what I mean. And this little white girl down in the Jacuzzi, well, she was about as anxious to try on a black dude as she was to pop pills. Well, what could I say? A poor black boy like me comin' out of the ghetto and all?" Lenny leveled his gaze directly at her and grinned broadly. "Tell you this much, the answer wasn't 'no'."

Wanda stared down at her black coffee. Her throat was constricted and her legs weak. She wanted desperately to run from the room but knew she would never make it off the couch. She found herself fighting the impulse to look again, just to glance at him one more time. He was playing with her, cruelly testing her sensibilities and trying to break her down. No man had ever tried that with her before, and it was a tough game to handle. She was determined to somehow be victorious.

"So . . ." Wanda began in a soft, weak voice, "her boyfriend came after you?"

"Yes ma'am," Lenny grinned. "Came right on after me. Should have gone after his girlfriend, not me. I didn't do nothin' to start that roll. No sir. Nothin'."

"Well," Wanda began again, "I have to make a report to the corporation on this matter. You . . . understand . . . of course, that they'll probably . . . ask . . . you . . . ."

She could not speak. Lenny had gotten to his feet and stood completely naked in front of her. His cock was growing, and he was smiling. "You understand the problem us black boys have, doesn't you, Miss Wanda?"

Wanda Morrison had seen two naked men in her life. Her husband and Harold. And neither had been the epitome of masculinity. Both with pale, flabby bodies and a definite inability to perform. Now, her eyes were locked into the sight of a beautiful body, lean and muscled, the manhood rising to gigantic proportions. The woman could not speak.

"You play a funny game, mama," Lenny said as he moved slowly toward her. "But any dude with any kind of sense can see that beneath it, you 'bout as hungry as any female could ever be. Just a matter of finding some dude strong enough to take what you got to offer."

He stood directly above her, the tip of his penis only inches from her mouth. Wanda stared at the pulsating flesh, her lips slightly parted and her eyes wide.

"Now," Lenny began again, "we just remove some of this jive costume you like to call business attire and get you down to the real lady beneath." Lenny reached down and gently took off her glasses, then removed the hair clip which held her auburn hair in the tight bun. Her thick mane fell luxuriously across her shoulders.

Wanda flinched as she felt her own hair against her flesh. She began trembling wildly as she felt Lenny's fingers at the buttons of her coat, then her blouse. Her arms were deadweight, and it was just a matter of Lenny raising them to remove the garments. She sat with only her bra and skirt, and Lenny quickly unsnapped the hooks and pulled the lacy underwear from her breasts.

"White skin . . . . " Lenny breathed as he bent down and took her hardened, pink nipple between his teeth. "White woman's flesh . . . ain' nothin' like it in this world."

From deep within her, Wanda felt the panic and the anger surge. She reached down and grabbed it, struggled to bring it to the surface. Like pulling herself from a bad dream, she began rising, feeling the surface come closer and closer. She finally reached the top and emerged.

"You bastard!" she screamed, throwing Lenny onto the floor with one hard strike.

For a moment, the shock got the best of him. But he was able to pull himself together quickly. He grabbed her arms, reached down and yanked open her legs. His hand moved quickly up between her thighs, and he tore at her panties. She was soaking wet down there, and Lenny knew he had it made. His fingers probed anxiously into the depths of tight pussy.

Wanda thrashed and screamed and bit, but the black man was too strong. She felt as though she were fighting herself as much as Lenny. The clothes were being ripped off her body, and Lenny's hard, lean body was pushing her down at every turn.

Finally, she lay naked beneath him. Her legs were spread wide, and as much as she fought, she knew there was no way of stopping him.

The fight was over. But instead of defeat, Wanda felt an overwhelming sense of ecstasy fill her limbs as Lenny's huge member entered her. Her body seemed to swell and ebb with each inch that invaded her moist cunt.

She cried and whimpered as he began pumping easily, then with increasing tempo inside her. Her body meshed with his, and she felt whole. Wanda Morrison threw her arms around the black man and pulled him closer, tighter against her own starving body. Wanda lay sprawled on the king-size bed, her nude body glowing softly in the morning sun. She was sleeping soundly, like a small child exhausted from the rigors of a hard day.

Lenny leaned against the dresser casually smoking a cigarette. In his hand, he held a Polaroid camera. Lying on the dresser behind him were a dozen photographs, all depicting Wanda in one position or another, all of them nudes.

Jason peeked into the room and grinned at the sight of the voluptuous nude woman on the bed. "Knew she was an animal," he whispered happily.

Lenny nodded. "Some kind of lady, Jason. Some kind of lady."

Jason glanced at his partner with a worried expression. "C'mon, man. Plenty of white heat roaming these parts. Don't need to concentrate all your energies on one."

Lenny grinned. "You worried 'bout me taking a headlong dive into some white muff, brother?"

Jason returned the grin. "Damned right, partner. We here for some good time, not to go messin' and fickin' up with no white women. Man, that's a death trip all the way down the line!"

"Man, I don't worry none 'bout no death trip. Fuckin' lames 'round here couldn't even kill themselves, even if they had to. Shit!"

"Shit nothin', brother. You just got yourself a dose of the golden hots! Next thing I know, you'll be up and marryin' that white bitch! Then what?"

Lenny raised the camera to his eyes, focused, and snapped another picture. Wanda moved slightly from her deep sleep but instantly fell back into it again.

Lenny turned to Jason and held him the camera. "Long as you're here, might as well make some use out of yourself, nigger."

Jason took the camera and removed the exposed picture.

"Just pull the trigger when I tell you, nigger." Lenny moved to the bed and dropped to his knees next to the pillow. He took his cock in hand and began rubbing himself until he was semi-erect. He moved the head around Wanda's mouth, and the woman parted her lips almost mechanically. Lenny gently stuffed his cock inside her mouth and turned back to Jason with a big grin on his face. "Now, brother, is the time!"

Jason snapped the photo. Lenny removed himself quickly from the bed. He picked up the photos lying on the dresser and began shuffling through them slowly.

"Why you taking them pictures, Lenny?" Jason asked.

Lenny grinned. "Let's just call it insurance, brother. Let's just call it insurance."

"I can dig it!" Jason laughed softly, slapping his partner's hand. "My doubts 'bout you gone, nigger. You just better than ever was is all! Just a whole lot better!"

Wanda Morrison continued sleeping as the two men laughed and left the room.

CHAPTER FIVE

LEXINGTON AVENUE in New York City was hot and humid. The stifling air had driven the black people from their homes and businesses onto the streets where they sat, sullen and angry, waiting for some gift. A natural breeze, a broken hydrant, a rainstorm. The kids played vigorously, and each game seemed to be drawn naturally to the corner hydrants. They had yet to break one open, but it was inevitable.

Churchman lay naked on his sweat-soaked sheets, the nude body of a black woman next to him. He listened to the street noises below, chain smoking one Camel after another. The presence of the girl had left his mind, he couldn't even remember her name. He had picked her up on the corner on his way home from a crap game, offered her ten dollars and she had nodded silently. That had been it, the way it was usually done with Churchman.

Women were not his specialty, at least the ones who

gave it away for free. Churchman knew from the beginning that he would always have problems. His face was scarred from a childhood accident, and his nose looked as though it had been punched deep into his skull. His eyes bagged, and his mouth was exceedingly large. He was, to say the least, ugly. And he knew it.

But human beings compensate for their drawbacks, and Churchman began compensating early in life. He was determined to transform his weak, flabby body into a muscled, well-oiled fighting machine. He began at the age of eleven and never stopped training. The word around Harlem was that a bullet would ricochet off his chest. The women spoke of him in terms of his body. "Get by the face and you got yourself a whale of a man," they would giggle. Of course, no one dared say this in front of the man who reputedly had devastated more human beings with his fists than many men had with their guns.

They called him Churchman because his mother, noting that he would never make his mark in normal socieity because of his incredibly bad looks, tried to get him into the ministry. Each afternoon, the ugly little kid could be seen tagging sullenly along behind his mother into the Lexington Street Baptist Church. The local minister had tried to help, but God and his domain did not interest the child. He wanted, more than anything else in the world, money and power. He could not accept the notion of a God, at least one who was just and kind, because no all-powerful being would have ever damned a human soul with a face like his. Churchman, whose real name was Lincoln Martin, knew there was no such thing as a sanctuary for him. He knew from the start that he would have to create his own.

The woman lying next to him began to awake, stretching her short, almost stumpy legs and spreading them widely. She was not pretty at all, her face was tired and worn, and although young she had the look of a woman who had spent long years on the streets. And in Harlem, that duty can age a human being fast.

"You alright, baby?" Churchman asked as she opened her eyes and smiled up at him.

"Just tired, and hot. An' I need something, honey, you know?"

He had noticed her flesh when she had undressed earlier in the evening. The pinholed roadmap of her private hell, the veins on her inner thighs, the marks running all the way up inside her legs and even to the lips of her vagina. She was obviously a heavy user.

"How much you need?" Churchman asked.

"Ten dollars, baby. Just ten dollars get me through this hell night."

Churchman nodded. He guessed her age to be somewhere around twenty-two, maybe even younger. He calculated that she would last until thirty, if that. The street below, which rang with the sounds of little black children shouting and screaming, produced nothing if not death. Lexington Avenue, he thought, creating the ugly sores of a beautiful white society, men and women whose early deaths were an almost certain product of their lives. There was no chance, only the killers survived because the game was life and death—from childhood on.

"I'll fix it for you, honey," Churchman offered after a long silence in which the girl awaited anxiously his decision.

"Oh babe!" she breathed, moving her hand down his belly and to his groin. He was instantly ready, and as her mouth traveled the rock hard stomach, Churchman closed his eyes and allowed his mind to cease functioning. Only the feeling remained, and they were both beautiful and for a brief moment in time, walked in the sunshine.

The harsh ring of his telephone interrupted his reverie. "Damn!" Churchman breathed.

The girl, her mouth firmly around him, reached up and grabbed his arm to stop him.

"You just keep happenin', child," he said. "This is probably business. Got to handle it."

He recognized the voice at the other end immediately. Churchman bolted upright in his bed, waved the girl off, and concentrated on the words emanating from the other end.

"Yeah, I'll be there," he said firmly, hanging up the phone slowly, a big grin spreading across his face.

"Good news, babe?"

Churchman looked at the girl and felt relief. From now on, it would be only the best for him. High-priced whores did not look at faces, only the number of bills in the hand. And it appeared, as a result of this one phone call, that he would have those bills.

"Got to dress, babe, and get my shit together. Churchman leaped from the bed and moved to his closet. He had one good brown mohair suit. Vested and cut with a continental flare, it served to create a stylish, elegant look while at the same time showing off his powerful shoulders and arms. It was the perfect kind of suit for his kind of work.

He dressed quickly, splashing on some expensive cologne and adding a touch of oil to his kinky hair. The girl sat naked on the bed and watched him, her eyes sad and cow-like. Churchman reached into his wallet and pulled out a twenty and a ten. "Here, babe," he said, handing the bills to her. "You need it more'n I do right now."

A wide grin broke out on her face as she examined the

money. "Oh man!" she cried.

Churchman regarded her for a moment. He had always had something for the weak. He hated them, and held sympathy for them. He had been one of them once, but now he was strong, both in body and mind. But it was difficult for him to forget where he had come from, especially with women.

"Don't mess the pad up too much, baby. I'll be back." He turned and left the apartment quickly.

The apartment on Park Avenue, directly across from Central Park, was everything that the tenement flat on Lexington was not. Clean, gracious and rich, it represented to Churchman the epitome of style and good living. He had met the man who lived on the tenth floor just once, an introduction made by an old crapshooting friend named Lincoln. The man had arrived at the game, held in an abandoned building in the Bronx, in a chauffered Lincoln Continental. He had exuded power then, with his fine silk threads and his gold-plated cane. No one knew much about him except that he was a powerful black man, risen from the streets and having made his money in drugs. The street dudes called him Sugarpops, but his name to the rest of the world was Carter Hodding.

Churchman walked past the old black doorman into the plush lobby of the building, then into the elevator. The stooped old man running the machine eyed him severely as they rode the ten floors to Hodding's apartment. Churchman stepped off the elevator and walked the richly carpeted floors to suite number 1011 and knocked lightly on the door.

A young black man, wearing an expensive suit and tie, opened the door.

"I'm Churchman," the huge, ugly black said in an even voice.

"Mr. Hodding's expecting you." The young black stepped aside and Churchman entered the apartment. The first thing that caught his eye was the view. All of Manhattan spread out beyond the huge window, with the mammoth trade center in full view. The night twinkled, the city looked beautiful. It was difficult to believe that in the streets below the people writhed and suffered with the pain of their nightmare lives. It was hard to conjure at the moment the image of the cheap little whore who had been with him throughout the day.

The rest of the living room was richly furnished with leather couches and chairs, modern paintings gracing the walls, and a fully stocked wet bar in the corner. A jazz station sounded mellow music over the stereo, and the soft lighting gave the room the feeling of a scene in a motion picture.

Churchman felt at home instantly. This was the kind of operation he was meant for. He had always believed that. And he was only twenty-six now, there was still time for him to achieve it.

A large man, in his early fifties with greying hair, stepped from the bedroom wearing a silk smoking jacket and slacks. He moved immediately to Churchman and held out his hand. "I'm Carter Hodding," he said as he shook Churchman's hand.

"Pleased, brother," Churchman said, noticing the power in the older man's grip.

Carter Hodding smiled. "Get you a drink, Churchman?"

"Sure. Anything."

"Fine. I have some twenty-one year old Chivas that should soothe the palate." Hodding moved behind the bar, took out two tumblers, added a few ice cubes and poured from an elegant-looking decanter. He handed the drink to Churchman.

"To your health," Hodding offered as a toast.

"And yours," Churchman replied.

"I've always wondered," Hodding began easily, "why they call you Churchman."

Churchman sipped slowly at his drink. "My mama, she always wanted me in the church. I guess she figured I was too ugly for the rest of the world."

Carter Hodding laughed. "All niggers too ugly for the rest of the world, Churchman. Just makes us all try harder."

Churchman smiled. He liked Carter Hodding, but was not deceived by the man's power. He had heard the stories revolving around Hodding's cruelty, his appetite for vengeance. Yet, at the same time, he was different from so many of the blacks Churchman had known. Elegant, kindly, almost like a grandfather. He had made it to the top without sacrificing his cool.

"You have quite a reputation, Churchman," Hodding said suddenly.

"I get around," Churchman replied.

"They say you don't carry heat. Just your fists are enough."

"I worked hard at it, Mister Hodding. Very hard."

Carter Hodding nodded. "They also say you're sharp. That you biding your time, waiting for the right strike."

Churchman chuckled. He had never heard that said about himself. Had never really given it much conscious thought. But, as Hodding mentioned it, it did seem to be what he was doing. "I guess so . . . ."

"That's good, Churchman. I like a man with patience, a man who knows how to wait it out. Ain't everybody on the same time schedule. With some people it comes later in life than for others."

Churchman nodded, finished his drink and allowed

Hodding to pour another. He was becoming anxious to find out why the man had brought him up here, why the richest nigger he had ever known was calling him in the middle of the night. Hodding was doing nothing but talking philosophy.

Carter Hodding moved to the couch and sat down. He looked directly at Churchman as he placed his drink onto the marble coffee table. "Now, for business," he said softly. "Please sit down."

Churchman took a seat across from the man and listened.

"You know two young blacks named Lenny and Jason, do you not?"

Churchman remembered the two from the streets. Smart dealers in everything from flesh to drugs, but too happy-go-lucky and too small time to be taken seriously. "Yeah, I know them."

Hodding nodded. "They left New York about a week ago. I believe they went to California. My contacts on the street told me they were talking about Southern California, like fools they had dreams that niggers would be accepted there."

Churchman continued to listen. He knew now what Hodding was leading up to, but he could not figure why. Two young punks from the streets of New York should not bother a man like Carter Hodding.

"I want those two," Hodding said finally. "I want them dead."

Churchman tightened the grip on his chair. He had actually hit only one previously in his young life, that being an old bookie who had skimmed a huge amount of money off an operator in New Jersey. Most of his work had been nothing more than throwing a few punches, or breaking a leg or an arm. A transcontinental hit was something totally out of his realm.

"The deal goes down like this," Hodding began. "Five thousand in cash tonight on acceptance of the assignment. A flight to the West Coast, a car will meet you at the airport, and accommodations in Newport Beach until the job is done. All expenses paid, Churchman. And five thousand more upon your return to New York City."

The deal sounded incredible. A few hundred here and there had been all that Churchman had come to expect from his employers. Small time compared to this man and his offer.

"But how will I find them, Mister Hodding?"

Hodding nodded. "Good question. California's a big place. All we have is the tip from Lenny's lady friend, and the fact that they drove cross country in a 1962 Cadillac Eldorado." Hodding reached into his pocket and pulled out an envelope. "In this packet is a description of the car, license plate number, engine number. Also, pictures of both men. Oh, and let me add that there is five thousand dollars in small bills, plus another two thousand for your first expense money."

Carter Hodding held the envelope out toward Churchman. The hesitation lasted for only a second, as the huge black man took it and slid it into his vest pocket.

"I'm glad you accepted, Churchman," Hodding said. "If you do this thing for me, and do it well, I promise you that things will be different for you when you return to New York. Do you understand?"

Churchman smiled. "Yes sir, I think I do."

Hodding stood and extended his hand. Churchman took it and the two men shook. "I must add," Hodding began, "that you will stay out there until you do finish the job. It's absolutely essential to me that neither Lenny nor Jason remain alive."

"I understand, Mister Hodding."

Carter Hodding led Churchman to the door and held it open for him. "My man Rick will drive you to the airport in one hour. He'll pick you up at your apartment."

Churchman nodded and started out into the hallway.

"Churchman," Hodding called after him, "in matters like these, a man never owes another man an explanation. But in this case, well, things might appear somewhat abnormal. Let me just say that the matter is personal with me."

Churchman looked into the wealthy black man's eyes. They were ice cold and deathly. Personal or not, the frightening gaze sent chills down Churchman's spine. "I understand, Mister Hodding," Churchman said before moving toward the elevator.

Carter Hodding watched the huge man move away from him. He felt satisfied that he had made the right choice.

She sat in the middle of the bed, still naked, with a rubber tube wrapped tightly around her thigh. At first glance it appeared as though she were playing with herself. But the sight of the needle, and the way she poked around near her vagina, made it plain what she was up to. She hardly noticed when Churchman walked into his apartment.

"My God!" he whispered as the young girl jabbed herself in that sensitive spot, drained the hypodermic, then fell backward onto the soiled sheets. When the rush had subsided, she stared up at the huge man with watery eyes. She smiled and spread her arms, then rubbed her kinky hair between her thighs.

"C'mon big daddy, mama alright now."

Churchman held himself rigid for a long moment. The girl became very soft now, her tension-ridden countenance seemed to dissolve into the soft lines of a woman. Her body, normally so tight and hard, seemed to mellow into the delicate curves normal for a mature woman.

"C'mon baby, please baby . . . ."

Churchman could not bring himself to do it. The woman was too fragile, too weak for him to move on her. Instead, he drew out the envelope which Carter Hodding had given him, flipped through the bills and counted out five hundred dollars. He lay the money down on the bed next to her.

"Got to leave tonight, sugar," he said softly. "But I expect to be back real soon. Keep the pad and yourself for when I get back, dig?"

She looked at the huge amount of money with wide eyes. Never in her life had she seen that much at one time. She picked it up and counted it out slowly. "Oh daddy," she moaned, clutching the bills to her breast, "you know I'll be right here, mellowed and waitin' on you."

Churchman leaned over and kissed her gently on the mouth. For the first time since he had picked her up earlier in the day, they kissed like lovers, gentle and probing.

"Remember, I'll be back any day. Then we'll party a little."

The girl smiled at him, put her hand to his cheek and began tracing the lines of his face. Churchman felt the pain which he always felt when a woman touched his face, and instinctively reached up and pulled her hand away. But the usual violence was not there. He was more gentle with her. "I'll be back," he said, then got to his feet and quickly packed his bags.

He left her sitting in the middle of the bed, holding the money to her breast, watching him. He knew the money had made a difference, yet there was something else happening which he could not understand. He would have time now to sort his feelings. He figured at least a week on the West Coast to find the two men Hodding wanted so badly.

As the 747 banked over the gleaming lights of New York City and headed west, Churchman sipped on his Scotch and though about the sudden change in his life. He was unsure about a lot of things, especially about Carter Hodding. He knew he was taking a chance, but for once in his life he would take the chance where a big payoff was possible. The girl's gentle, almost loving reaction to his money earlier had convinced him of the fact that he could not survive this world without money. Enough money to buy the love of at least one woman. And if he had to find and kill two young punks from New York City to achieve that, then he would. Anyway, he decided, the questions were insignificant compared to the emptiness at the pit of his stomach he had lived with for twenty-six years. It was time to fill the well, no matter the cost.

CHAPTER SIX

AT THE SAME MOMENT the huge 747 lumbered off the runway at Kennedy in New York, the party in the recreational room of the Palmwood Gardens apartment complex was just getting underway. Sponsored by the apartment's social director, a gee whiz former cheerleader who still believed in high school dances and proms, the party immediately took on a more ribald air than the director had anticipated. A disco sound system had been rented for the huge room, and a wet bar complete with bartender put in to use.

But the guests, many of them outsiders, came for only one purpose in mind—sex. The girls wore string bikinis, some of them so skimpy that they might as well have been nude. The men carried quaaludes and vials of cocaine, ready to induce the pretty nymphs into whatever activities the drugs could buy. The social director watched as the guests began arriving, and with hands on hips stormed from the room. She had titled the party a "get to know your neighbor" event, a welcoming affair to summer and new friends. She had not intended it to be an orgy. But the stage had been set early by the guests, and control was lost.

Upstairs in their apartment, Lenny and Jason were putting the finishing touches on a few lines of coke. Using the gold-trimmed mirror and the silver-plated straw which he had acquired in New York City, Lenny worked at the dining room table evening out the white powder and getting the four good-sized lines in order.

Both men were dressed in their finest casual wear, tight fitting slacks with expensive silk shirts opened to the waist. Lenny wore a gold chain with a coke spoon dangling from the end. "Better to advertise a little of the wealth," he had explained to Jason after the latter objected to the necklace because he felt it was too obvious.

"Okay, my man," Lenny smiled, putting the razor blade back into the black leather pouch which was his coke kit. "Best we snort some of this shit 'fore it blows away."

Jason took the silver straw, bent over the mirror and snorted a line. He threw his head back, sniffed the powder in deeper, then did the same with the other nostril. Lenny picked up the straw and finished off the last two lines.

"This and a little of that Jack goin' make us non-stoppable niggers tonight!" Lenny exuded after snorting the coke.

"Best there be some foxes want some of this shit. Hard enough traveling all the way up to L.A. to score it."

"Goddamn, man," Lenny scowled. "Every white cunt on this coast do 'bout anything for a little coke. It's the nature of California."

"Hope so," Jason grinned, stroking himself obscenely. "Old junior down here ain't had no work-out since last night. He's achin' for love!"

Lenny laughed at his friend, then finished off the remaining whiskey in his glass. "You just don't worry your black head about nothin', partner. The L.A. trip was well worth while!"

It had taken Lenny and Jason exactly one afternoon to secure a cocaine connection in the West Hollywood sector of Los Angeles. Borrowing Wanda's Buick sedan, they had left early in the morning, spent the day cruising Hollywood, and finally settled on the seamy, yet expensive ambience of West Hollywood as a likely place to score. With all the stylish boutiques, shops and strange little discos, the place seemed like a natural for two young blacks to get in touch with the right man. And the man they had found was the type the Hollywood chamber of commerce tries to make the outsider believe is not representative of that neighborhood.

With long hair, tight fitting jeans and watery blue eyes, Hank, as he called himself, made it known very quickly that he would like nothing better than to trade off his coke for a little black ass. But his business sense had quickly overcome his homosexual desires, and Hank had sold Lenny and Jason five grams of the stuff for the price of four hundred and fifty dollars. The stuff had been cut with procaine, a local anesthetic which numbs the nostrils, but aside from that it was some of the best coke either Lenny or Jason had ever had.

The trip had been easy, the most difficult part being when Lenny had to return the car to Wanda. He had begun visiting her at least once a day at her swank Newport Beach apartment, but she had wanted more. She had even given him some money, money that eventually went for the coke. And she was getting possessive, like a desperate woman hanging onto the bare threads of a dissolving mariage. Lenny had found it necessary to slap her around a little before leaving, making it known to her exactly what the situation was.

But once back in Palmwood Gardens, with their five grams secure in their coke kit, the night was wide open. They had seen some of the white girls making their way into the party, most of them wearing bikinis with towels draped across their pearly white breasts.

As Lenny had said, "Fresh cunt, fresh courage." Not that either needed courage, but it was always good to keep a healthy supply on hand.

"Well," Jason said after finishing his drink, "let's get our black asses down there and boogie!"

"Yeah, man, it is definitely party time!"

The lights in the recreation room were soft, and interrupted only by the pulsating verve of the strobes. The music was loud, a base beat reverberating throughout the room. Couples danced in the center of the room as though in a trance. The girls who wore bikinis seemed as though they were nude beneath the soft lighting. Their bodies writhed and moved with the music.

"Holy Jesus, my man," Lenny exuded, staring at the bodies on the dance floor. "This place is too fucking much!"

"Won't be long, brother," Jason chortled, " 'fore those lily white ladies begin strippin' off those expensive little triangles they call bikinis. No sir!"

"Best move we ever made, bro," Lenny added.

Jason looked at his partner, their eyes locked deeply for a moment. "We had to, Lenny. Ain't no choice in the matter."

Lenny continued to grin. "Don't matter a shit, partner. They still three fuckin' thousand miles away, wondering where the hell we got our black asses to. Ain't no problem."

Jason nodded. "Guess the last place they look for two back street dudes like ourselves be some swank apartment complex in Orange County. I mean, any nigger with any sense at all would get his ivory ass far away from this kind of scene as possible."

"Now you're cooking, nigger." Lenny slapped Jason on the back and pulled him into the center of the room. Two white girls, both blondes, were standing near the bar, wearing tight little bikinis and sipping on exotic rum drinks.

Lenny approached them easily, wearing a big grin and doing a little of the shuffle. "Hey ladies, what's happenin'?"

The girls looked to each other and giggled. The taller of the two turned away from her friend to Lenny. "Just trying to get high," she said eagerly.

Lenny turned to Jason and shrugged his shoulders. "Man, you hear what these fine ladies sayin', partner? They sayin' they tryin' to get high! Man oh man, with everythin' flowin' round here, I ain't never hear no such jive shit in my entire life!"

Both girls began laughing. The taller one seemed very taken with Lenny. "You know what?" she asked.

"I know everythin', lil' darlin', 'cause that's the

name of my game!"

"You sound just like J.J. Walker on 'Good Times'."

Lenny broke out laughing, and Jason followed quickly.

"Goddamn," Lenny chortled. "Ain't never been complimented like that 'fore in my entire existence. No sir!"

"But you do, you really do!" The girl was no older than eighteen. She wore a knitted string bikini which revealed the rounded flesh of her breasts almost to the point of being nude. Her belly was slightly rounded, and her legs were long and lean. Her girlfriend was shorter, and much heftier, but still exhibited a sensuous, firm body.

"Well, goddamn, Jason, you hear these two young fine things, talkin' 'bout me sounding just like a movie star. And 'sides that, looking to get themselves high! Goddamn, Jason, what you suppose we ought to do?"

Jason shrugged. "Just so happens me and partner just made a hefty score of some of the pause that refreshes, if you ladies can dig where I'm coming from?"

The girls looked quickly at one another and smiled.

"Coke?" the tall one asked.

"Ain't Pepsi," Lenny replied.

The two girls huddled together in the living room of the apartment. Lenny sat at the kitchen table, once again preparing the cocaine.

"Now you know," Jason said, speaking seriously, "that in Harlem, when the bloods get together and do some of the Bolivian powder, it is customary for everyone to get naked."

The girls smiled weakly.

" 'Course, that's only tradition," Lenny added quickly. "Makes us feel closer to the natives who had themselves one hell of a religious experience behind the stuff. The brothers feel might close to those natives. We feel that we inheritors of the earth, the jungles, the mountains . . . ."

"That's a truly beautiful thought," the tall blonde said.

"Yeah, far out," her friend added.

Lenny shrugged. "Just that when you natural folk like ourselves, you got to align yourself with the other natural folk from around the world. White man sometime forget that. 'Course, girls like you, seeing as how hip you are and everything, you understand that notion pretty good."

The two girls nodded. Their light blue eyes were fixed on the huge pile of cocaine which Lenny was preparing. Both he and Jason could see their mouths watering over the sight.

"So," Jason began, "if you girls don't mind, I'm going to follow tradition handed down through the dark ages by brothers like ourselves."

Both girls watched with astonishment as Jason began taking off his clothes. When he was naked, they gasped but could not take their eyes off him.

"There is tradition in everything we brothers do," Lenny commented casually as he separated the line and made the coke ready. "Those who follow those traditions with us, well, we consider them one, you dig where I'm coming from?"

Whether or not they fell for the line did not matter to either Jason or Lenny. They had the girls coming and going. On the one side was the lure of the cocaine, a sure way to any modern girl's heart. And on the other was the worship of the white girl toward the black man. Either one of these factors, both men knew, would lead to some good times.

The tallest girl smiled as she pulled off her top, then

stepped easily out of her panties. Naked, she was like a little girl. Her pubis was so light that it appeared as though she had no hair down there at all. But her large, firm breasts were strong evidence of her womanhood.

When her friend followed suit and stripped, she presented a much more sensuous image. Her pubis was dark and full, and her breasts, although small, possessed alrge, luxuriant nipples.

Jason and Lenny stared at the two visions of Southern California beauty for a long moment. Jason grew instantly excited, and both girls seemed fascinated by the almost immediate rise in his nature.

"Okay, lil darlin's, come get your candy." Lenny sat back as the two naked girls hovered around the table, taking the straw to their noses and sniffing the stuff energetically.

"Taste good?" Lenny asked.

"Far out," the little one said.

"Yeah," her friend agreed.

When Lenny and Jason had taken their tokes, the four nude partygoers walked hand in hand into the bedroom. When the tall one asked what was going on, Lenny shrugged and replied that it was just another part of the "ritual."

The party had moved out of the recreation room and into the Jacuzzi. There was hardly a square foot of water space left as white body upon white body writhed and squirmed beneath the bubbling waters. Jason and Lenny stood above the group, watching what seemed like a ritual water dance with fascination.

"You think anybody know anybody by name?" Lenny asked with a grin.

"Appears it make no fucking difference, brother,"

Jason replied.

They had left the two blondes upstairs in their apartment with a couple of lines of coke and some sore flesh. The girls had been very cooperative, the magic of the Bolivian powder had worked its small miracle. After having their fill, Lenny and Jason had decided to return to the party and see if they couldn't broaden their horizons a little with some new recruits from the Jacuzzi.

The party had moved to the hot pool. Bodies were squeezed into the small area like sardines, with everyone holding a drink above their heads to make sure it wasn't diluted with chorinated water. Jason and Lenny stood above the mass of humanity, looking down into the swirling water for something approachable. They had figured on the way down that possibly Debbie and Kris would be available for a little party, but neither of the girls were present. And Don and Peter, the two blond thugs, were also absent.

"Hey, Jason, Lenny!" the shrill voice carried above the laughter and voices of the others in the pool. "Over here!"

Sylvia sat alone in the far corner of the pool. The top to her bikini was off, and she waved gaily in Lenny's and Jason's direction.

"Place loaded with white fox, and we got to land an old broad."

Lenny slapped his friend on the back. "She got the thing for you, brother. It's obvious for any man to see."

Jason shrugged. "Shit, Lenny," he muttered.

"Go on, my man. She supposed to be rich and everything, use some of that talent the Lord give you and make some coin. I mean, we set ourselves up in this lame jungle right, we never have to work again. You dig?"

Jason looked back to Sylvia. He decided that she wasn't really all that bad. Her breasts were not young, but neither were they terribly old. Just a little sag, but a lot there to keep a man interested for a while. Anyway, he decided, if Lenny were right, there would be money there.

"Jason, come on down here."

The moment he climbed into the pool she was all over him. Her hands were up between his legs, she pushed her breasts against his chest, and pulled one of his hands down between her legs. Jason grew excited immediately. It wasn't the fact that she was beautiful that turned him on, but the fact that she was aggressive. What he and Lenny had been playing off on, their black flesh amidst white skin, was obvious now. This woman did not go after him with subtlety, but with wide open desire. And it was exciting.

"You're the finest specimen of a man in this entire complex," Sylvia whispered feverishly in his ear.

Jason kept his hand firmly between her legs. He peered over her shoulder and saw the looks on the faces of the other bathers. Some of the young girls were open-mouthed and wide-eyed. He could sense that the scene which he and Sylvia were putting on excited them. The men, however, possessed a different look altogether. Their mouths were tight and their eyes cold. They lay back against the side of the pool with a look that said, "Okay, nigger, show us what an animal you really are."

"C'mon," Sylvia said in a begging voice, "let's go up to my place. Okay?"

"Sure thing," Jason agreed. Happy to get away from the stares of the white people. Lenny had disappeared somewhere, and without his friend Jason felt very much alone.

Sylvia lived in a one bedroom in the wing behind the tennis courts. She had turned her apartment into what could be termed an orgy room. The living room was filled with huge Arabian cushions, hanging plants and soft, indirect lighting. The room reminded Jason of an expensive whorehouse which he and Lenny had once gone to in New York City.

"Like a joint?" Sylvia asked after closing the door behind her black stud. Jason nodded, and watched the woman pad half nude across the living room floor to the kitchen. She opened a drawer and pulled out a silver serving tray loaded with rolled marijuana cigarettes. She lit one nervously, took a long drag, then handed the joint to Jason.

"It's Colombian. The best there is."

Jason nodded as he took the pungent smoke into his lungs. Another lame, he thought to himself, feeling the rough scratch of the smoke on his throat. The shit was, at best, Tijuana backyard grown, nothing more. The fine grasses did not burn on their way down like this particular stuff did. He decided that the woman was something of a fake.

But Sylvia was the kind of lady who lived in her own dream. She had enough money to support herself without working, and enough lack of inhibition to turn her life into a sexual sideshow. She was one of those women who, when reaching that mystical middle-age, drop all pretenses and blatantly go after what they need to satisfy their lusts. In a strange way, Jason admired a woman like Sylvia. At least she didn't play games with her desires, and didn't use her age to prey on the innocent. Any man who stepped into her apartment knew exactly why he was there and what was expected of him.

The grass, although not the best, was at least mellow. Combined with the cocaine still in his system, it produced a very nice effect. Jason threw himself down on the cushions and smiled up at the older woman.

Sylvia stood above him, her thumbs hooked into the elastic of her bikini panties. She knew how to light herself so that the telltale lines of middle age were softened. She actually looked young now. And, she had made an attempt to keep her body in condition. Her legs muscles looked strong, and she had a solid belly. "You like to look at white women, don't you?" she whispered.

Jason grinned. "Yeah, baby, long as they treat me right."

Sylvia pulled on her panties, bringing the top down as far as the upper line of her pubic hair. "I treat all my boys right, Jason. No one walks out of here without some special favors."

"You talkin' my lines, baby," Jason replied. "Man can't just play all the time without thinking 'bout his future."

"Take off your clothes, Jason." Sylvia gave the order without sounding dominant. It was a request, an excited plea.

Jason obliged. When he was naked, he watched her eyes hungrily devouring him.

"My God, you're beautiful," Sylvia breathed softly. "Am I beautiful, Jason?"

"You're fine, mama, just fine."

Sylvia parted her lips slowly, then ran her tongue across them. She began sucking air in, making soft whistling sounds. As she did this, she slowly pulled off her panties, stepping out of them with a small stagger. She was obviously a lot more drunk than she had let on. But she did manage to keep herself in some kind of control.

Standing nude above him, Sylvia began putting on a show. She spread her legs, and drew her hands slowly up between her thighs. She began playing with herself slowly, rhythmically, as Jason watched her writhing belly with hunger in his eyes.

"You like?"

Jason nodded. He reached up and stroked her belly, then allowed his hands to glide across her white skin to her mound. Sylvia thrust herself out to him, letting his fingers invade her moist sex.

As she dropped to her knees in front of him, she took his erect penis into her hand and held it firmly. She examined the huge black staff closely, like a small child examining a Popsicle.

"I've never seen one before," she said softly.

"A prick? You never seen a prick?"

"No, silly. A black cock. I've never seen a black cock before."

Jason laughed softly. "Well, does it live up to the stories?"

Sylvia nodded eagerly. She leaned down and put her lips to the tip, using her tongue to stab at the hole. When she withdrew, she looked up at the dark face staring down at her, an almost bemused look in the eyes and a sardonic scowl at the corners of the mouth.

"I'm a typical white bitch, eh?"

Jason laughed out loud.

"I mean," Sylvia began in a flood of emotion, "I'm as racist as everyone else. I'm just driven by more hunger than other women. I've never had one before, and I wanted one. Does that insult you?"

Jason eyed the woman intensely. He had taken note of the way she had toyed with the white boy who had been at her side a few nights ago. The kid had been putty in her hands, trained like a dog to whimper and crawl and beg at her every command. Obviously she had been used to men like that, had organized her life around the notion that all cocks could be bought. It was different now, however. She was deferring to something that seemed to be eating her inside. Maybe it was guilt, Jason speculated. Maybe the race thing did bother her to the extent that guilt overrode her carnal desires. If that was the case, he decided, he would have to assume control of the situation, and of her.

"It does insult you, doesn't it?" Sylvia offered again, still stroking him gently.

Jason reached down and grabbed her by the hair, pulling hard enough to cause momentary pain, Sylvia's eyes watered, and she gasped. But a small, long suffering smile crossed her face.

"It does insult me, white bitch," Jason said, bringing his voice as low and mean as he could. "You look at a black man as though he were an animal, some kind of jungle freak. Like you watch the baboons at the zoo playing with themselves all the time, and secretly you dig on how groovy it would be to have one of them horny beasts in the form of a man. A big, juicy hard-on whenever you needed it. A prick without a mind attached so you didn't have to jive with no games."

Sylvia looked up at him with a glazed expression in her eyes. Jason still held her hair, and she his cock. She wanted to hear more.

"And then," Jason began again, "you jive around thinking 'cause you put those white lips to black meat you doin' the world a favor. That the dude gettin' his dream come true. That we all sittin' 'round thinkin' Nat Turner dreams of white castles filled with white skin. That white pussy better'n black pussy. Truth is, bitch, white bitch want the black cock more'n black man want white pussy. Always been that way!"

Sylvia was breathing hard now, her voice had become a soft memory of what it had been a few moments ago.

"Anything, Jason, anything you want . . . ."

Jason smiled. He put his hands on her head and pulled her forward between his widespread legs. He could feel the hot, moist breath between his balls. She put her lips to the sac and began using her tongue.

"Lower, baby," Jason ordered. "I wanna be clean just like a white man."

Sylvia obeyed. She had never done it this way to a man before. Always, it had been the men doing it to her. And Jason smiled as her tongue wormed its way inside him. He knew he had her where he wanted her.

CHAPTER SEVEN

LENNY HAD LEFT HIS PARTNER with the older woman, knowing full well what would follow. His senses had told him early on that there was something to be gained by his and Jason's association with the older women of Palmwood Gardens. Wanda, for instance, had seemed well off and ready to try something new. And, they already knew what Sylvia's scene had been. With the right amount of play, Lenny knew that both he and Jason could develop a situation that would prove highly lucrative.

As he watched Jason leave the Jacuzzi with the topless older woman, Lenny lit a cigarette and ducked into the shadow of a palm tree beneath the building. It was a warm night, and the cocaine was just starting to wear off. He felt mellow and excited at the same time. It seemed as though the action never stopped, and the fact that every time he turned around something new was brewing gave him an energetic thrill. He and Jason were having a better time of it than they had supposed, and it looked as though it would never end.

"Lenny?" the voice called out from behind him. It belonged to a girl, and Lenny thought he recognized it. He turned back to the shadows and saw the shoulder length blonde hair, but little else.

"Lenny, it's me, Kris!"

Lenny took a long drag of his cigarette and sighed. One moment of solitude and it had ended quickly. There was no getting away from the action.

Kris waited for him just inside the hallway. She wore a skimpy string bikini which covered very little of her voluptuous body. She smiled nervously as Lenny approached her.

"Hey baby, what's happenin'?" Lenny grinned.

Kris moved her weight from one foot to another. Her eyes darted around Lenny, up and down the hall, then back to him. "I just wanted to see you," she said quickly.

"Well, that's cool," Lenny said evenly. "But why the hassle?

"It's just . . . well, you know, Don."

"Oh, yeah," Lenny mused. "Big bad Don. Tried to lay me out in the hallway the other night. Man got to be crazy comin' down on three niggers like that."

"He's insanely jealous," Kris offered. "I guess he has reason to be, though."

The girl took Lenny's hand and placed it on her breast. She closed her eyes and swayed a little as Lenny tweaked her hardened nipple beneath the fabric of her bra. "Oh, Lenny, just that once wasn't enough."

She was a beautiful white girl, there was no denying that. Her breasts were about the most beautiful that Lenny had ever seen. Firm and upturned, they were almost perfect.

"Come upstairs, babe," Lenny offered. "This place is wild, but not wild enough to accommodate making love in the hallways."

Kris smiled, then placed her finger at the base of his neck and slowly moved it down across his chest, belly and groin. Lenny shivered when she grazed the tip of his cock. "Okay, upstairs," Kris whispered.

They moved quickly to the elevator, then rode to the third floor. The hallway was empty, and Lenny pulled the girl to his room. As he inserted the key into the lock, he heard the footsteps behind him. He tried to turn around and fling out with his leg, but it was too late. Before he could move, big Don had his neck in an arm lock, with his muscled forearm directly against his windpipe.

"One move, nigger, and I bust it," Don said in a low, mean voice.

Lenny did not move. He could feel the strength of the big blond and knew he would be a dead man if he did move. He turned his eyes to the side and looked at Kris. She looked up at him helplessly, then turned away. Lenny could tell that she was feeling shame.

"Okay, open the fucking door!" Don breathed.

Lenny unlocked the door and suddenly Peter appeared out of nowhere and kicked it open. Don pushed Lenny into the living room and kicked the door closed behind him. Using his foot as a lever, he threw Lenny across it and onto the floor.

"Okay, nigger, looks like we even the score a little." Don was dressed in Levis and a flowered shirt. With his blond bangs and his hugely muscled body, he gave the appearance of a totally deranged man. Lenny had always been wary of the white man, but had had little chance to really fear him. In Harlem, there just hadn't been that many dealings with Caucasians. But now, staring up into the black, powerful faces of Don and Peter, he did feel fear.

"Kris," Don ordered, "fix us a drink."

Kris looked down at Lenny, then to Don. She turned and half ran into the kitchen.

Don sat on the edge of the couch, while Peter stood guard next to the door. Folding his arms in front of him, Don grinned almost idiotically down at the black man on the floor.

"What you dudes want?" Lenny asked finally.

Don looked to Peter and shook his head. "Listen to that nigger, would you? Jungle bunny wants to know what we want. Well, let's just say school's in session, jigaboo. Let's just say you're about to learn what the white man feels about gutter shit like yourself."

"Listen man," Lenny began, "I ain't done nothin'. Just tryin' to live, party a little, like you dudes." Lenny knew that everything he said would be twisted and convoluted until it fit into the white man's thought patterns. But he had to try something, had to stall them off as long as possible. There was the chance that Jason would return, and the two of them against the white boys would have a chance. And, then again, there was always the possibility that Thadius would stop by for one of his nightly beers. If those two failed to show, Lenny knew, he was in for a beating.

Kris served drinks to Don and Peter, then went back into the kitchen. Almost automatically, she started washing the dishes. Lenny had to keep himself in check because he was about ready to laugh at the ironic gesture.

"First things first," Don began after draining half his drink. "Where's your stash?"

Lenny shook his head slowly. "Sold it all this mornin'," he said slowly.

Don stood up, towering over the black man, and kicked Lenny hard in the stomach. Lenny groaned and rolled onto his back. Don then raised his foot and placed it firmly on Lenny's groin.

"One more time, nigger, the stash!"

Lenny had no doubt the man would do it. If he had a machete, he would've used it to slice off his balls. Lenny waited until the pressure became unbearable.

"The icebox," Lenny said finally. "In the cream cheese."

Don nodded to Peter, who moved quickly to the refrigerator and pulled out the foil-wrapped cheese. He sliced open the package and found twenty one-gram vials filled with white powder. "It's here, Don," he said excitedly.

"Bring it over, Pete. Let's test it."

Lenny felt his heart sink as he watched the two men slobber over the cocaine. That was at least two thousand dollars worth of the stuff going into their hands. White nostrils would take it now, and they would laugh and fuck behind it, knowing they had stolen it off a stupid nigger. And Lenny was angry about that. He had been stupid, taking Kris up to the apartment after all that had gone down between himself and her boyfriend. Once again, as it always did, the white man was prevailing. And these two jokers, Lenny thought, were morons. And yet, they were winning tonight.

"Good shit," Don said as he sniffed in a huge spoonful of the coke.

"Hardly cut with anything," Peter quipped, grinning at his friend.

"Nigger's lucky he's got such good shit around here." Don grinned down at Lenny, then raised his foot one more time and placed it on Lenny's groin. "Okay, the other stuff. Pills, grass, whatever."

Lenny shook his head violently back and forth. "I ain't got nothin' more."

"Bullshit, man! You sold Peter here a hundred of the motherfuckers, ripped him off plenty for 'em too!"

Lenny shook his head again. "No man, they all gone!"

Don released his foot. "Okay, cocksucker, we're going to search this place. We find one lousy pill and you'll never fuck again. You got my drift?"

Lenny felt a chill screech up his spine. Ordinarily, a threat like that was just that, a threat. But this situation was different. The man was angry for a number of reasons, but primarily because of the fact that a "nigger" had made it with his girlfriend. It was simply the worst thing a black man could do to a white man. And Lenny figured the man was angry enough to destroy his manhood.

"Under the bed mattress," Lenny said quickly.

Don grinned down at him. "Now you're thinking, ace. You be a good boy and you might even get out of this intact."

Lenny nodded.

He listened as Peter threw the mattress onto the floor. Then Peter let out an enthusiastic yell and came running into the living room, carrying two metal boxes. "Must be thousands of 'em here!" he shouted.

"Well, well," Don began. "Looks like you cooperated nicely."

Lenny waited. He knew it wasn't over, and he knew he would have to suffer through whatever they were on the verge of giving him. But the odds were stacked against him at the moment, and his only chance was to wait it out, stay calm until he could muster his own resources and return the favor. He wondered if the white boys were totally crazy. If they were planning to leave

Southern California with his stash, then they would survive. But if they intended to stay anywhere in the area, they must have realized that Lenny would come after them. Their only sure out would be murder, but Lenny had figured that neither man had it in him to kill in cold blood. He hoped he was right.

As Don and Peter drooled over the stash which they had confiscated, Lenny turned to look at Kris. She was standing at the bar next to the kitchen, leaning on her hands, watching the two men as a mother would her children. She sensed Lenny looking at her and returned his glance. Lenny could see that as far as she was concerned, the score had been evened. There would be no more trouble, her boyfriends were satisfied. Lenny tried shaking his head, a gesture he hoped would indicate to her that not everything was completed. But Kris just nodded in return.

"Okay, nigger," Don began after putting away the pills and the cocaine. "Looks like we got almost all of what we came for."

"C'mon, Don, let's go," Kris said suddenly.

Don spun around and glared at the girl. "Shut your fucking mouth," he cursed.

"Please, Don, we've got everything."

"I told you to shut the fuck up!"

Kris turned away from him angrily. She lit a cigarette and puffed on it nervously.

"Seems like the chick still has the nigger hots," Don said to Peter.

Peter nodded. "Sure does, Don."

"Can't have that, can we?" Don growled at Lenny.

Lenny knew it was coming. He started to pull his knees up to his chin to give himself as much protection as possible, but it was too late. Don struck out with his foot and landed a blow at Lenny's stomach.

"God man, no!" Lenny shouted.

"Fucker!" Don screamed back, generating his own momentum as he began lashing out with more powerful kicks. He struck Lenny in the ribs, then in the shoulder and once again in the stomach. The last blow convulsed the black man, and he felt his insides begin to churn. He couldn't stop the sickening churning of his stomach, and let go with a huge stream of vomit. The stuff splattered Don's pants leg.

"You fucking puke over me again, nigger, and I'll kill you! I swear!" Don's voice reached an alto octave, screaming almost like a woman. His body shook and his movements became uncontrolled, like a small child wailing out at his pillows in anger. Lenny feared this reaction more than anything. He knew the power which the man possessed was great, and he knew that Don did not have much of it under control. It was dangerous as hell, because while Lenny knew Don did not want to kill him, he knew it was possible behind the lunatic rage which the white man now exhibited.

"Nigger! Nigger! Nigger!" Don half jumped, half ran around Lenny, kicking him in an almost comical dance. But the blows were hitting their mark. Lenny could feel his ribs burn, his stomach convulse and his shoulders give way beneath the beating.

The only fortunate aspect of the moment was the fact that Peter did not participate. Lenny knew that if tried to stop the madman above him, then Peter would jump into the fight. The two of them against himself would have been disastrous.

Lenny gritted his teeth and held himself as loosely as possible against the onslaught. Blood spurted from his mouth, and his entire body felt as though it had been broken. He stared at the looming figure above him, his senses reeling and vision blurred. In the far recesses of his consciousness he could hear the shrill, girlish voice screaming at him.

Then, suddenly, it stopped. Silence reigned throughout the apartment. Lenny lay in the middle of the floor, a small pool of blood near his head, and tried to focus his eyes. He saw the three figures moving hurriedly toward the door. He listened as the door closed. Now, there was total silence.

Lenny tried to move. He tested each part of his body. His fingers moved slowly, one blow had struck his hand and Lenny was sure that it was broken. Next, he moved his legs. The soreness had already began to set in. His stomach muslces were tied up in a knot, and his shoulders were aching. Slowly, he sat up and braced himself against the dizziness which accompanied the effort. As he staggered to his feet, he held onto the edge of the coffee table and slowly began focusing on the hallway which led to the bathroom. With great effort, he made it to the washroom, turned on the faucet, and stuck his head beneath the cold water.

The bottle of Jack Daniels was still sitting on the kitchen counter. Lenny took a couple of swigs, felt the liquid numb his senses, and thought about what he would do. The anger had begun swelling inside as he pulled himself together. At first, he had been grateful to be alive, but as each moment passed, he became more and more outraged. The lames had dealt with him as a nigger, and for the moment, at least, they had won. And Lenny knew that if he went after them now, he would become a victim once again, this time to the white police and their so-called justice system. No, there had to be another way, another avenue to pursue in the white man's paradise. His thoughts turned immediately to Wanda. For the moment, at least, she was the most powerful person he knew. And her power was less than the power which he held over her sexual appetite. Lenny smiled to himself as he drained off another couple shots of the whiskey and made plans to pay Wanda a visit.

Harold sat on the edge of the bed with his head hanging down, his flabby hands cupped weakly between his knees. Behind him, Wanda lay naked and smoked a cigarette. She wasn't angry, nor did she feel as though she had been denied. She had long ago resigned herself to Harold and his "moods" as he liked to call them. In the beginning, they had affected her badly, making her feel unwanted and very old. But as time went on, she had become accustomed to him and his ways.

"The pressures," Harold said weakly, trying to suck in his flabby belly. "I've been under a lot of pressure."

Wanda exhaled slowly. "I know, Harold, it can't be helped, a man in your position." She laughed to herself as she uttered the latter. Harold was going nowhere in his profession, and he was the last to realize it. Coddled as a child, given everything by his parents up to and including a second mortgage on their house in order to put his way through an expensive yet little known law school, Harold had always been the kind of man who expected things to be delivered to him on a silver platter. Even his own manhood, Wanda thought to herself.

"It's going to be different," Harold said, turning to the nude woman next to him. "Just as soon as I finish this case, I'll be out from underneath."

Wanda chuckled. "Like the last time, Harold?"

"I know what you're thinking, Wanda. It isn't true."

Wanda raised her eyebrows in shock. She knew what he was referring to. He had discussed the subject before. It always amused her because it seemed as though he spent more time wondering about his sexual predilections than why he was so wound up that he couldn't perform. But with Harold, she knew, the image was all important.

"Listen Harold," she began in a soft voice, like a mother speaking to her child, "I know what you're going through. Believe me, it doesn't bother me." She stroked his flabby shoulders, and once again felt a strange revulsion at the man's lack of tone. His body was pale, his muscles underdeveloped as though he had lived his entire life sitting and waiting. Harold had never found joy in athletics and his body showed it.

Wanda patted him on the head and got off the bed. She walked nude into the well furnished living room and stood in front of the huge window overlooking Balboa harbor. The night was beautiful. The houses across the bay twinkled their lights upon the still waters, a few boats moved lazily down the channel. Her apartment was on the third floor, and it afforded her a fantastic view of the beautiful harbor and bay.

She heard Harold moving around in the bedroom. She knew he was getting dressed. The script would play the same, she thought. He would pull out the bottle of gin, mix himself a martini, and smoke mentholated cigarettes until they were pouring out of his ears. He would sit at the dining room table, the alcohol producing a vague melancholy in him. His voice would become strained, almost to the point of choking sobs. His round face would turn the color of a pale crimson, and his light blue eyes would become washed and unseeing. His entire focus would be upon the inner sadness and self pity which he felt. Harold, Wanda knew, had always wanted to be great, but greatness, even normal success, were not to be his. It often made him cry like a baby.

He hardly noticed her nude presence as he moved, almost gracefully, to the kitchen. With a weak smile, he pulled down the gin and began mixing the martinis.

"Like one, Wanda? May do us some good."

Wanda nodded. Of course she'd like one. Might as well get plastered since nothing else was going to happen. She turned to Harold, still naked, and smiled. "I feel like really getting drunk!" she laughed.

Most men would have lost control, having a beautiful naked woman standing over them desiring nothing more than getting drunk. But Harold could only nod solemnly. His weight was too much to allow for any real sexual excitement.

Ironically, he toasted their relationship. "We have a long way to go," he said softly, "but we'll make it."

Wanda sipped at the cold drink and absently rubbed herself as she felt the gin warm her body.

"Why don't you put something on so we can talk?" Harold suggested as he noted where her hand had gone.

"Of course, Harold. Don't want to get too excited, do we?" The anger in her voice was unmistakable. The night was a warm, clear one, and Wanda had felt exceedingly sexy. As a matter of fact, since her encounter with Lenny she had found it difficult to return to her life of sterile passion. She had even begun to masturbate in the middle of the night, which was something totally out of character for her. Yet, the feelings which had begun to surface within her were, on the whole, not undesirable.

Wanda returned to the kitchen wearing a see-through negligee which did little to cover her nudity. Her firm, well-proportioned body seemed to glow beneath the smooth fabric. The shadow between her legs became even more inviting. But Harold was having none of it. Instead, he hung his head over his martini and fiddled with an extra long cigarette.

"Someday," Harold moaned, his voice choking, "someday it'll happen to me. I really believe that."

Wanda nodded, half listening, as she poured herself another martini. The drink was making her body tingle, and she could not stop rubbing her nude thighs together beneath her gown.

"I'm much more talented than all those others," Harold continued. "I've got much more to offer."

"They're just jealous," Wanda offered, her voice containing a teasing ring to it. "They don't want to move you too fast. That's all."

Harold shook his head back and forth. "I expected to be so much further ahead at this stage of my life. I expected to be there."

Before she could ask him where "there" was, the conversation was interrupted by a loud, urgent knock on the front door. Harold jumped as though someone had set off a firecracker next to his chair.

"It's only the door, Harold," Wanda giggled.

Harold looked to her with plaintive eyes. He did not want anybody or anything to destroy his private and pitiful reverie. Harold had always hated parties just for that reason. He felt he could not communicate properly with a lot of people in the room. One shoulder, and one shoulder only to cry on.

Wanda went to the door, pulled the latch and peered out into the hallway. She gasped when she saw Lenny standing there.

"I need help," Lenny said quickly. His face was puffy and caked with blood. He held his left side as though attempting to hold the tissue and bones together. Wanda could see that he was staggering, as if from a blow.

"Lenny, I . . . ." Wanda began quickly, turning to Harold. The pale man sat hunched over his drink waiting for her return.

"Please, baby, I ain't in no mood to stand out here and jive."

Wanda knew the problem she was creating, but opened the door anyway. The way things were going with Harold, it didn't make much difference what the man thought.

Lenny staggered into the apartment and stopped short when he saw Harold. His streetwise mind summed the man up instantly. Just the way he was sitting and the obvious flab on his body convinced Lenny that the only way he would ever be able to hurt him was with his mind and his power. Physically, he was no threat whatsoever.

"Uh, Harold, this is Lenny. He's one of the tenants at the Gardens."

Harold tried to pull himself together, but the effort was too much for him. He nodded up at Lenny, his pale blue eyes focusing on the young black man.

"What happened to you?" Wanda asked.

"I got rolled. Two white dudes came into my pad and beat the shit out of me."

Wanda touched Lenny's ribs and Lenny groaned. "The same ones as before?" she asked.

Lenny nodded.

Harold swigged down the remainder of his martini. Anger was beginning to replace his sorrow. Wanda was still dressed in her see-through negligee, and Harold noticed Lenny's eyes moving across her nudity.

"I think this is a matter for the police," Harold said suddenly.

"Harold's a lawyer, Lenny."

Lenny nodded. "Yeah, okay. But I can't go to the police. See, them dudes ripped me off for some grass. And I'm a black man living in a white man's apartment complex. Don't think the pigs would listen too long to my sad story."

Lenny was sharp enough to know what the California laws relating to drugs were. Marijuana, less than an ounce and for consumption only, was nothing more than a misdemeanor. Anything more was a felony. Lenny hoped that he was walking the line with Harold between the two, allowing the man to understand that there was more involved than just an ounce of grass.

But Harold did not understand. He cited the law to Lenny regarding marijuana possession. "See, there's no problem," Harold said, as if speaking with a child. "Now why don't you just go to the police and clear this thing up."

Lenny looked to Wanda and rolled his eyes. "I can't go to the police, Wanda," he said softly. "You know that."

Wanda glanced up into Lenny's coal eyes, then turned quickly to Harold. "He's right, Harold. There's a lot of tension at the complex right now. It would be difficult."

Lenny watched the other man's hands carefully. He had learned in the streets to keep his eyes on a man's hands. They usually foretold his mood. Harold's hands at the moment were clutching the martini glass, his knuckles were white. The small, pudgy fingers reminded him of a baby holding onto his rattle.

"Well goddammit," Harold began, his voice pitched high, "you've no right to come in here and ruin our evening!"

"Sorry, man," Lenny said, his voice low and very cool. "I was in trouble and needed someplace to go."

"But why here?" The plaintive cry in Harold's voice pierced the growing tension in the room.

Lenny looked down at Wanda, allowing his eyes to move to her full, nude breasts. A half smile crossed his lips and he shrugged. "Guess 'cause she's the only friend I got," he said simply.

Harold was becoming livid. He rose to his feet, breathing heavily, and threw the martini glass at Lenny. It hit the black man's shoulder and bounced harmlessly to the carpeted floor. Wanda quickly knelt down and picked it up.

"Now get out of here!" Harold screamed.

Lenny turned to the man with a scornful twist to his mouth and shook his head menacingly. "You sound like a fuckin' woman, man," he said ruefully.

A short cry emanated from Harold's lips. "You goddamn nigger bastard!"

"Harold!" Wanda cried.

But it was too late. Lenny leapt across the table and had Harold by the throat. The chubby white man folded beneath Lenny's powerful grip, and he became quickly nothing more than pure dead weight. Lenny could not sustain the weight, and dropped him to the floor.

"You fucking nigger! You goddamn fucking nigger!!!" Harold lay on his back, kicking out at Lenny with his chubby legs and screaming.

Wanda was becoming hysterical, and begged both men to stop fighting. Lenny stood above the man and placed his right foot on Harold's stomach. "You apologize, fat man, or I'll break your goddamn balls, if you got any to break!"

Harold watched the foot as Lenny moved it down across his belly and to his groin. When he felt the pressure on that area, he began crying. "Wanda, please, help me, Wanda!"

Wanda turned away. She could watch no more. For the years and months she had gone out with Harold, the man had stood precariously on the edge of her tolerance level. Her respect for him had died long ago, and only because he was a convenience and was non-threatening had she agreed to continue seeing him. Now, this exhibition of pure cowardice was revulsing her. She felt like vomiting over him, showing what he really meant to her. Instead, she turned away.

"Lady don't help no man who begs and cries, honkie!" Lenny said as he exerted more pressure.

Harold whimpered, then began really crying.

"Apologize, cocksucker," Lenny intoned again.

Between sobs, Harold apologized. Lenny immediately removed his foot from the man's belly and stepped back.

Slowly, Harold got to his feet. He tried to straighten his clothing but his hands were trembling so badly that he found the chore virtually impossible. He resigned himself to his rumpled shirt, and turned to find his jacket. He put that on, then walked up to Wanda.

"Wanda?" he begged.

Wanda remained with her back turned to him. The horrible wail of his voice was intolerable. She could not listen to another word. "Get out, Harold," she muttered.

"But Wanda . . . ."

She turned on him with an anger that he could not have foreseen. "I said get out, you impotent little cocksucker! The day you think you can make a woman feel like a woman, then try coming back! But not before!"

Harold was crushed. He moved slowly toward the front door. Wanda watched him, feeling pity and anger at the same time. She knew, however, that someday, somehow, Harold would latch onto another sucker to cry to, someone else to listen to his painful, sobbing odyssey of life as she had done for the last couple of years.

When the door closed behind him, Wanda took a

deep breath. She felt suddenly as though a huge weight had been lifted from her shoulders.

"I'm sorry, babe," Lenny said casually.

"It doesn't matter, Lenny," Wanda replied.

Lenny smiled, opened his arms and welcomed her into them. He felt her nude body push against him as she opened her mouth to his.

"You sure everything's cool?" Lenny asked.

Wanda rested her hand on Lenny's groin and smiled. "This," she said, tracing the outline of his erect penis, "makes everything alright."

Wanda curled up against Lenny's lean, strong body and sighed. The night, for her, had been at long last fulfilled. He had been brutal with her after Harold had left, but it had come exactly at the right moment. She had been craving it all night, and Harold had not delivered. Lenny had. It was as simple as that.

"Feelin' alright, baby?" Lenny asked as he lit a cigarette.

"Beautiful," Wanda sighed. "It's never been like that for me before."

"That old boy Harold don't look like he could jack off let alone take a woman like she need to be taken."

Wanda laughed at the image of Harold trying to have sex with himself. "Harold's very into himself," she said.

"He's a fucking pansy is all. Little white boy think the world owes him somethin'. He wouldn't last no time in the streets."

"I know, Wanda sighed. "It scares me sometimes to think about that. I mean, if Harold ever had to do an honest day's work."

Lenny laughed as he passed the cigarette to Wanda. She inhaled deeply. "Are you feeling better, Lenny?" she asked.

"Yeah," Lenny nodded. "You always make me feel better. Only thing that hurts still is my pride. Those damn white boys beat the shit out of this here nigger, and that hurts worse than any kind of pain."

Lenny waited anxiously for Wanda's response. When there was none, he spoke again. "It's tough to walk into white man's land like we done. Me and Jason, two niggers up for grabs. And now this. Man," Lenny sighed, "I figured it'd be different than New York."

"Is that why you left the East?" Wanda asked.

"Yeah. It got real hot there. White men killin' blacks, blacks killin' whitey. Everybody after somebody's life. Whole fuckin' town gone mad. Me and Jason, we just figured we had to get ourselves some peace 'fore we die. Decided California was the place. Guess it ain't so."

"It hasn't been all that bad, has it? I mean, tonight, okay, that was awful. But for the most part, the people at the Gardens have been friendly, haven't they?"

Lenny nodded. "Yeah, they been alright. But one thing like what came down tonight . . . well, it just fucks up the whole thing."

Wanda sighed. "I know what you mean. Maybe there's something I can do about it."

She looked anxiously at Lenny, but he turned away.

"Lenny?"

"Hey," he replied coldly, "ain't nothin' no white woman can do for no nigger. I take care of my own business, you dig?"

Wanda was becoming excited. She threw herself against him, clutching at him. "Lenny, don't be stupid! Talk like that will get you nowhere. The Morris people will have you out of there in two seconds if you start anything!"

Lenny laughed sardonically. "That's the whole fuckin' point, ain't it, baby? Jive motherfuckers throw me out on my ass for defending myself while them white boys run around scot-free beatin' up on black men. Shit!''

Wanda pulled herself away from him and sat up in the bed. Lenny had a point. He was instructing her into the realities of the corporation, the realities of white America. She was asking this man to back down only because he was black, and for no other reason. Clayton Manchester, the president of Morris, had already called her about the two black men. His voice had been dry and laced with anger, but he could not express himself accurately. All he wanted to know was what the potential for trouble was with the two blacks living in Palmwood Gardens. He had discussed the NAACP with Wanda, explaining the potential for real trouble from them if something happened. The bottom line had been that they were locked into the situation, and there appeared to be no way out. They would have to keep the "Negroes" whether they liked it or not. Wanda had agreed. There had been no discussion of simple human rights or decency, just straight business talk about the effect of Lenny's and Jason's presence on the clientele as well as the NAACP. At the time of that call, Wanda had not felt that they were dealing with a man, a flesh and blood human being with feelings of his own. Instead, they had been dealing with an entity, a presence that could harm the business if not handled properly. Kind of like an insect which could be controlled only by an insecticide that would also kill the plant itself.

Now, Wanda was beginning to see the situation differently. She had opened herself to this black man, he had taken her dormant sexuality and brought expression to it. He was no longer just an abstract issue, but a man. Wanda knew now that she would have to do something to help him in a real way.

"Maybe there is something I can do," Wanda said softly.

Lenny looked at her inquiringly.

"No," Wanda answered, returning his look. "I don't mean fighting your battles for you. I mean, something about ridding Palmwood Gardens of the kind of hoodlum that beats up on people. I could do that, I think."

Lenny shook his head. "Know something, I'd be about ready to accept that. Never thought I would, either. It's just that if those two turkeys hang around much longer, I know there's gonna be trouble."

Wanda leaned over and kissed the black man. His cool flesh sent shivers of excitement throughout her body. "I'll try to get them out," she whispered. "It's just good business, Lenny."

He took her violently into his arms and lay her down across the bed. Wanda spread herself easily to him as he moved above her. She watched his every move like a hungry young girl just beginning to learn the secrets of love.

CHAPTER EIGHT

CHURCHMAN SAT BY THE WINDOW overlooking Balboa harbor and stared out at the blue-green waters. He smoked one cigarette after another, and occasionally sipped from the tumbler he kept filled with Scotch.

California had been like a dream from the moment of his arrival four days earlier. The skies had been washed clean of smog and haze by a gentle wind from the deserts to the north. The Los Angeles basin spread out below the airplane like a green fantasyland, dotted with the blue sparkle of swimming pools. Never having been out of New York City, Churchman had marveled at the sight. He had thought it the most beautiful thing he had ever seen.

The sweet smell of sage had greeted him as he stepped off the plane, the gentle warm winds were clear and soothing. If someone had set the stage to seduce a newcomer to the city, they could not have done a better job than that which was done on Churchman. All the girls in the airport were pretty, and they moved easily with their cut-off Levis, bra-less tee shirts and beautiful tans. Everywhere the black man looked were beautiful people, toned by the sun and mellowed by the breeze. For the first few hours in Southern California, it was difficult for him to connect his deadly mission with the beauty around him.

Only the arrival of Clinton Jones, a dour black man in his late forties, maintained the reality of Churchman's visit. Jones had been waiting outside the airport terminal in a used Lincoln Continental. He had approached Churchman with a slow gait. He was dressed casually, with beige double knit slacks and an open collar print shirt. It was in his face that Clinton Jones betrayed his alienation. He did not belong with the beautiful people of the sun.

"Carter Hodding sends his regards," Jones had said, extending his hand.

Churchman shook hands and looked at the man intensely. Jones was a workhorse, a lifer who had paid his dues in the streets for the better part of his existence. He was not smooth, but neither was he rough. He was a corporate man, content with the small jobs and the smaller money. Churchman sensed that his greatest attribute was his loyalty and his willingness to carry out any order.

They drove in silence toward the Santa Monica Freeway, then into downtown Los Angeles. Hodding had rented a room at the Hilton on Sixth Street for Churchman.

"Carter decided it would be cool if I showed you around a little," Jones said as the skyline of Los Angeles loomed some fifteen miles ahead of them. "This town can rack your brain if you don't know what's coming down."

Churchman had been wary at first. The plan had been for him to simply pick up a car, then pursue the contacts which Hodding had given to him prior to leaving New York. The presence of Jones was unexpected.

"You got yourself a nice room at the Statler Hilton. There's a short waiting there for you."

Churchman nodded. "Any messages from Hodding?"

Clinton Jones smiled. "Just like in the cowboy movies, you got to get your man."

The room at the Hilton had been small, and furnished cheaply. Churchman was disappointed. He had felt that the job called for a first class ticket all the way. At least, he thought to himself, the man had the decency to leave a bottle of Chivas Regal on the small coffee table by the window.

Clinton Jones quickly took the bottle and began pouring drinks. "We've already got some information on those two niggers for you," he said calmly as he handed the drink to Churchman.

"Is that right?"

"Uh huh. Used our contacts out here, namely the junk yards here and down south. Seems that the Eldorado they used to cross the country fell apart once they got here. They junked it down in Orange County, a big yard run by a brother in Santa Ana."

"How did you find that out?" Churchman asked.

Los Angeles and its surrounding areas had impressed him tremendously. The land mass was tremendous, it seemed impossible that a man could do business on the street the way he did in New York. There was just too much space, too many territories to cover.

"They got a communications network in them yards that's wild," Jones grinned. "We just got on the horn and asked around about the car. The date it was junked was about the same time as when them two dudes should have arrived in California."

Churchman sipped slowly at his drink. "So where does that leave us?" he asked.

"Well, bro," Jones began, "inside the short were some pamphlets and a rental agreement for a pad in a place called Palmwood Gardens. That's a big white man's swinger paradise south of here near the ocean. Apparently them two dudes got white pussy on the brain. Don't think no niggers ever been in that place."

"So what are we doing here?" Churchman asked.

Jones chuckled as he waved at the room. "This is only for the night, my man. Let you get rested and shit like that. Tomorrow morning, we drive down to Newport Beach and set you up in a motel. And then, you're on your own."

Churchman nodded. He liked the idea of spending at least one evening in L.A. He had heard a lot of stories about the place, and he wanted to see some of it firsthand.

"So," Jones grinned, "you get yourself put together and I meet you in about an hour. Got a couple of fine numbers lined up, we'll go do a little bit of the town."

The girls were just that, fine. One, who was Churchman's, was a beautiful little woman in her early twenties. She was soft and light skinned, and had a strong, wiry body. Churchman knew they were paid-for hookers, but it didn't matter. Just having a beautiful woman like Jana come on to him erased the set up behind the evening.

Clinton Jones seemed to know the city well. He took them to the Sunset Strip to a couple of shows, then to Scandia restaurant for a late dinner, and on into downtown near Watts where a couple of all night jazz concerts were in progress. At each stop, Jones would pull Churchman into the restroom and take out his leather cocaine kit, complete with three full grams of the stuff. It was fine shit, and Churchman enjoyed himself thoroughly.

The following morning, Clinton Jones drove Churchman south to Newport Beach. It was a pleasant drive, and when they reached the seaside resort town the weather had turned spectacular. The warm winds continued, but were laced with a cool breeze from the ocean. And the people, Churchman had never seen people as beautiful as those who walked the streets near the ocean. They were like a different race, white men and women with perfect bodies, sunbleached hair and the look of absolute health. The girls were all young, some looking like they were in their early teens, but they were all beautiful. It was definitely a land of milk and honey.

"You got to learn to concentrate hard when you're in California," Clinton Jones laughed as they stood at a crosswalk waiting for three bikini-clad dreams to cross the street. "Man just go crazy with all this fine white pussy running wild out here. And these girls don't give a shit. I mean, they got to pass laws making it illegal for them to run around naked. Otherwise, no one would wear clothes. The fools!"

"They sure don't look like New York babes, do they?" Churchman offered as they continued down

Newport Boulevard.

"Shit no!" Jones replied. "Fine sun out here, plenty of good, healthy fruit. Man, these kids are like from another planet. Don't know how fucking quick they are, seem like most of them retarded or something. But who needs to be quick when you look that good?"

It was an odd sensation for Churchman as he rode past these beautiful creatures. For the first time in his life, he didn't feel particularly ugly. There was absolutely no way he could begin to compare himself with these young white gods and goddesses so there was no way he could come to the conclusion that he was ugly. It was as simple as that. And it made the black man feel good.

Clinton Jones had picked out a small motel overlooking the harbor. It was called The Seaside Inn, and Churchman's room was on the second floor with a beautiful view.

"Think this ought to fit your style, man," Clinton smiled as he opened the drapes onto the scenic bay below.

"It's cool, Clinton," Churchman said slowly. As much as Clinton had attempted to show the man from New York the better side, Churchman had begun having odd feelings about the whole situation. He wasn't positive about where those feelings were originating from, but there was undeniably something churning his gut. Possibly it was the slow pace of California that bothered him. Or maybe it was Clinton himself. Churchman had never been on a job like this before and had no idea, at the outset at least, of what to expect. The streets of New York had induced within him a hyper sense of movement, and he found it difficult to remove himself from that pace.

"We got your short downstairs," Clinton said as he watched Churchman unpack his one suitcase. "New

Caddy. Beautiful wheels."

Churchman felt the other black man's eyes on him and turned away. More and more, Clinton Jones was beginning to bother him. "You going to show me the apartment where I can find my men?"

Clinton Jones nodded. "Right away, my man. Problem there is security. They pretty tight in those complexes. You'll probably have to spend some amount of the time checking the place out."

"And we don't know for sure if they're there, do we?" Churchman said suddenly.

"Nope. That's why you out here, my man. You the one who going to find out, and take care of the business."

The two men sat outside the front entrance of the Palmwood Gardens apartment complex. The long white Cadillac did not look conspicuous amongst the Porches, Lincolns and other Cadillacs parked out front.

"Well, this is the place," Clinton said after a silence.

Churchman looked the facade over carefully. Two glass doors leading into what appeared to be a huge lobby. Around the side, there was a small path wandering into the tropical foliage consisting of palm trees and thick bushes. Two young women, dressed in white tennis outfits, suddenly emerged from that pathway and walked quickly to a new Mustang. They glanced at the two black men sitting acros the street.

After the bottle had been drained, and the sun was setting over the quiet waters of the bay, Churchman decided that he would think no more about his feelings. He would concentrate solely on the job at hand, nothing more.

Carter Hodding had seen fit to supply his New York mechanic with a suitable set of casual clothes proper for the Southern California environment. Clinton Jones

115

had left the suitcase of clothing in the motel room. Slowly, Churchman began sorting through the garments—light-colored double knits, print shirts with huge collars, sneakers and a pair of suede casual shoes. Churchman tried on a few of the outfits, and finally selected a pair of beige slacks, a white shirt and the suede shoes. It was amazing what the change in clothing did for him. His general appearance seemed to modulate almost instantly into that of a well-to-do young black, instead of a frightening thug from the streets of New York. The change made Churchman laugh.

The lobby doors to the complex were open, and Churchman walked casually through the front entrance of the apartment complex. The plush setting, the multitude of pool tables to his left, the soft lighting all impressed him. It was difficult to believe that normal people lived like this, the splendor which he saw had been reserved for only the rich. Maybe in California, he thought, everything was different.

The young woman standing at the reception desk eyed him suspiciously as he moved past her. He smiled at her, and she smiled back. He knew that if his two targets were the first black men to live in the Palmwood Gardens complex, then his presence would raise some kind of speculation. But he felt that with his clothes, and a quiet attitude, he could pull it off. There was also the fact that as soon as the job was finished, he would catch a plane and disappear into the tangled jungle known as New York City. The peering eyes of the whites in this apartment complex would never look up him again.

The main courtyard was quiet, except for a few people swimming in the huge pool. Churchman walked casually by, looking down at the shimmering bodies of two girls who tossed a ball back and forth. Beyond was the Jacuzzi, and a group of people sat huddled together at the far end talking quietly amongst themselves. They stopped talking as the large, well dressed black man sauntered by. Churchman could feel their eyes devouring him. He wondered almost idly if the snub-nosed .38 he carried in his shoulder holster was visible. Casually, he brushed his hand against his jacket, making sure the weapon was properly hidden.

Beyond the Jacuzzi were the dark alleyways between the apartments themselves. Churchman moved into the twisted maze and walked slowly. As he moved through the huge complex, he drew a map of the place in his mind for future reference. If it turned out that his men were not here, then he would erase that map and go on from there. If Lenny and Jason, however, did still live here, then he would need the map.

The rental receipt which Clinton Jones had secured from the junked Cadillac did not have the apartment number on it, only the date. Two and a half weeks ago Lenny and Jason had rented a place here. But for men on the run, two and a half weeks was a long time. Churchman knew that they could be almost anywhere right now, possibly even in another country. But this was his only lead, and he had to follow up on it.

Churchman continued walking through the complex, passing young white people wearing bathing suits or tennis outfits. They would glance at him quickly, then go on about their business. Churchman had decided that the place was so huge, filled with so many people, that there was no way the tenants could have known many of the other tenants. Thus a new face, even one belonging to a black man, could pass through without raising too many eyebrows.

Just as Churchman was about to turn into 'F' complex, a voice called to him from his rear.

"Wait up a sec, bro," the voice called out.

Churchman froze. His right hand moved slowly up the front of his shirt, within hoisting distance of his .38. He turned slowly toward the source and saw an old black man wearing the battle gray uniform of a security guard. Churchman could see instantly that the only weapon the older man carried was a huge flashlight, one that would double as a billy club.

The guard approached Churchman slowly. "What's goin' on, my man?" the guard asked.

Churchman smiled. "I guess I got myself a little lost. Come all the way from 'Frisco lookin' for two partners down here. Lost their apartment number when my suitcase was lost." Churchman spread his hands in front of him helplessly as he grinned sheepishly. "Had to buy these threads real quick like. 'Frisco ain't got the weather you folks do down here."

Thadius looked the man over carefully. He looked like a football player, or at least a man who had done a lot of playing in his youth. His broad shoulders, fine physique and broken face attested to the fact that the man had spent many hours using his body as a weapon on the turf.

"You ever play any ball?" Thadius asked suddenly.

Churchman grinned, not unused to the question. "Sure did, my man. Ran a little with the Juice up at 'Frisco State before he made his move to S.C."

Thadius beamed. His main passion in life was football, and O.J. Simpson his greatest hero. "When was that? '65?" Thadius offered.

"That's right, my man," Churchman bellowed. "Me an' O.J.! I was his blocking back for that whole year. He became a millionaire and I went into insurance."

Thadius was completely taken, at least for the

moment. "Must have been somethin', though. Playin' beside a man like O.J.?"

"Greatest ballplayer ever, my man," Churchman said. "Good man, besides. Ain't never been nobody like him, never will be. A straight ahead dude from the word 'go'!"

Thadius beamed as he shook his head slowly back and forth. "Damn shame 'bout his leg this year," the old man said.

Churchman took his cue. "Spoke with him 'bout two weeks ago," he began confidently. "Was talkin' about retiring from the game because of that damned leg. Asked my opinion on the matter, and I told him I couldn't decide something like that for him. It was up to him."

"That's wise," Thadius agreed. The guard continued to smile and shake his head. "Man like that, he come once in a lifetime."

Churchman agreed. At first, he thought the old black man was playing along, trying to feel him out. But as they talked further about football, and ran down the teams for the upcoming season, Churchman realized that the man was lonely and bored. He was one of those people ready to believe anything as long as it made his own life more interesting. The truth about people had long deserted him as a main consideration. His only goal had come to be avoiding death through boredom.

"Listen, my man," Churchman began, "I'd like to continue rapping with you, but I really got to find my partners."

Thadius nodded, the smile disappearing from his face.

"But I got an idea," Churchman bellowed. "The Rams practice out in Fullerton. Why don't you come along with me a week from Saturday? I'll introduce you to some of the players."

Thadius was delighted with the idea. "Man, oh man, sounds beautiful!"

"Outasight," Churchman bellowed again. "Catch a scrimmage, then go out for some drinks and a steak."

Thadius was overjoyed. He took Churchman's hand and shook it enthusiastically.

"Okay, pick you up here at noon, week from Saturday," Churchman said.

"Fine. Fine." Thadius repeated over and over again.

Churchman turned and started to move away but stopped, snapped his fingers in the air, and turned back to Thadius. "Shit, almost forgot! My partners, Jason and Lenny? You wouldn't happen to know which pad they in? Save me a lot of hassle up front."

Thadius grinned. "Only two niggers in the joint besides me. Nice dudes, too. Maybe they want to come along on Saturday?"

Churchman grinned. "Ain't no way they'd miss it, my man!"

"Try apartment E-319," Thadius said. "And if they ain't there, they be down in the Jacuzzi picking up on some young stuff."

Churchman laughed. "Shit! Them dudes ain't changed at all. Same shit as always!"

Thadius watched the big man disappear into the F building and smiled to himself. It seemed like suddenly his life was turning around, that he was meeting the kind of people he had always wanted to know. The boredom which had scarred his existence for so many years was suddenly evaporating and was being replaced by a good feeling of activity. He felt suddenly very young again, and was enjoying the feeling throughly.

Churchman walked quickly past the door which was numbered E-319. He checked out the hallway, the fire exit at each end, and the general location of the room. From his studies outside he knew the room overlooked the Jacuzzi and had a balcony. He decided as he moved quickly down the stairwell that it would be difficult to get them inside the room itself—the noise and the escape would be almost impossible to handle. He also knew that his presence would be discussed by the old guard, and that he must move fast. He figured that he would have mo more than twenty-four hours to make his move. Twenty-four hours in which to murder two men—and for what reason he did not know.

CHAPTER NINE

JASON STOOD OVER THE KITCHEN TABLE and grinned down at the money lying in the center. "Two hundred fifty, my man, just for fucking!"

Lenny laughed. "It ain't right, Jason. You supposed to be payin' her for a little something. Not this way."

"That old broad so horny, Lenny, she sell her soul just to get laid. I mean, she come down with this jive about her being a patron of the arts. Imagine that! Old foxy babe wants some black cock and she got to invent all these stories."

Lenny nodded. "Everybody around here is crazy, Jason. Everybody. Last night with Wanda, man, that was something else. She got this fag for a boyfriend don't know he's queer, which makes him even queerer. Wanda so hot between those legs she don't know whether she coming or going."

Jason picked up the money, folded it neatly and stuffed it into his pants pocket. "So what did she say about them dudes who rolled you?"

"Said she'd get 'em out of here." Lenny lit a cigarette and drew heavily on it. "But I don't know, my man. I'd sure like to get a few licks in there before those cocksuckers split. They still got all our stash. That about two months worth of high living being carried around in their white hands."

"Well, listen, brother, whatever you want I'm with you. You dig?"

Lenny grinned. "I know their car. They drive an old Pontiac, white one. I know where they park."

"Well, what you say we pack our rods and go down there and sit it out? Jason was smiling, the thought of getting back at the two white thugs was pleasing to him. "I mean, they got to get their shit together sooner or later. And if we wait 'em out down there, probably be no witnesses. We get our stash back, and return a few unanswered favors."

Lenny nodded his agreement. "I was hoping you start thinking my way, Jason. Figured you might not want trouble since you got yourself this money-paying love life of yours."

Jason laughed. "Shit, she'll be there waitin' with legs spread and that hot pussy of hers till the day she dies. Bet even then she gets herself laid by the undertaker. That woman was just born to have some cock inside her!"

Lenny rose from the table. His ribs still hurt from the night before, and his stomach muscles ached. "Okay, my man, let's start our waitin'. Figure Wanda probably talked with them dudes this morning, so they probably packing their shit right now."

"Okay, let's get them rods and get down there!"

The underground garage ran the length of the entire apartment complex. There were two levels, both underground, and both filled with the cars belonging to the tenants. In recent years, Thadius had been instructed, along with the other security guards, to patrol the garages because of the alarming number of rapes that had occurred down there. The presence of the guards, however, hadn't stopped the rapists from attacking the pretty young girls who lived in the complex.

When Lenny and Jason entered the garage, however, the cavernous concrete structure was empty. Only the cars remained. Lenny led his partner down the center aisle to the last space next to the wall.

"There she is, brother," Lenny said, gesturing to the used Pontiac.

Jason ran his fingers along the rear fender of the car as though he could divine something from the action. "White motherfucker'll have one hell of a time driving this piece of shit when we get done with them."

Lenny snickered softly. "Goddamn right, bro. And we be back in business, if they got any of our stash left."

The two men sat down behind the car to begin their vigil. Both carried small .22's, but neither man expected to use the weapon. They knew that they could take the two white boys, as long as the contest was one on one. They had discussed their attack earlier, and both agreed that the last thing either wanted was to waste the white men—all they were after was to even the score.

An hour passed, then another. Finally, halfway into the third hour they heard footsteps on the concrete, then voices. Lenny peered over the trunk of the car and saw both Don and Peter walking quickly toward them. The two boys carried suitcases and seemed upset. They kept glancing back over their shoulders, as if expecting someone to be following them. But there were looking in the wrong direction. When they reached the car, they stopped short. Lenny and Jason stood on the other side, grinning, and pointing their .22's at the two men's faces.

"Don't try nothin' funny, motherfucker," Lenny said in a low, mean voice. "Lest of course you want your fucking white skulls blown across this parking lot!"

Both raised their hands over their heads after dropping their suitcases to the concrete. Their normally tanned faced turned instantly pale, and their light blue eyes seemed to turn even a lighter shade of blue.

"Hey man," Peter began in a quaking voice.

Lenny cut him off with a wave of his gun. "Don't 'hey man' me, you white motherfucking cocksucker! You dudes come in two at a time and mess with me like that! You don't come around and 'hey man' me after that! You dig where I'm coming from?"

Both men nodded.

"Now," Lenny began in a much calmer voice. "It appears to me that you two lames got but one chance to walk out of here alive. And I suggest you take that opportunity."

"You listen to my partner," Jason added. "He offed more dudes than you cats care to think on. Dig?"

Lenny could detect a slight trembling in Don's hands. He could also see the man attempting to swallow, but it was obviously quite painful and difficult with his dry throat.

"Now," Lenny began again, "there are things here which should be evened up, dig? But I been out on the streets long enough to know that fighting don't solve nothing. Could easily put an eye out on both of you cats right this minute without killin' you, but that wouldn't solve nothin', now would it?"

Don and Peter shook their heads anxiously.

"Any suggestions how I might recoup my losses from

last night?" Lenny asked, a wicked smile crossing his face.

Peter looked to Don, and Don to Peter.

"Shit, assholes!" Lenny shouted. "You idiots got two angry, mean niggers with guns pointed down your throats and you still got to think about it!? Man, oh man!!!" Lenny was half laughing as he spoke. "You turkeys are really funny," he added.

"Listen, man," Don spoke, his voice pitched high, "we still got the shit—the pills and the coke. Right here in the bag."

Lenny turned to Jason. "Hear that, brother?"

"Sure do, my man. Surely do."

"Them boys still got our stash, and it appears they going to be nice enough, not to mention smart enough, to give it back. Life sure is nice, ain't it?"

Don started bending over to open the bag, but was stopped by the ominous sound of Lenny cocking his pistol. "Wouldn't do that, my man," Lenny said softly. "Leastways you want that head of yours to remain on that body!"

Don blanched and straightened up. He held the bag out to Lenny. As he opened it, he began smiling. The coke was there, and so were the pills. Lenny began counting the pieces. "Well, one gram of coke done gone from this here bag," Lenny said sorrowfully.

Don nodded. "We did it up last night. We'll repay you for it."

"Street price about a hundred dollars right now," Lenny said cheerfully. "You boys got a hundred?"

Both Don and Peter shook their heads.

"Well, ain't that a shame. Goddamn, and I thought we could even up the whole score here, be friends again like we were last night before you motherfuckers got it into your lame heads to rip off this here nigger."

126

Lenny turned away from his captive audience for a moment, shaking his head slowly and pondering the situation. Jason held his gun on the two men. No one moved.

"Goddamn," Lenny began in a soft, almost friendly voice. "I still hurt from that beating I took. But I figured it was just business and if I could get my stuff back, well, then, I might just forget the whole thing. I mean, who's to say I wouldn't of tried the same thing had I been in your places."

Don and Peter waited with almost childlike eagerness for Lenny's words. They nodded with each point the man made.

"See, gentlemen," Lenny began after a short pause, "on the streets, you'd both be dead motherfuckers right now."

Lenny waited for this to sink in, then continued. "But this ain't the streets, is it? I mean, we in some apartment house with a pool, lots of pussy, and good times. People just don't expect to die in a place like this. Do they?"

Almost like idiots, Don and Peter nodded their agreement.

"Shit," Lenny added, "I guess nobody dies in Palmwood Gardens. You white folks seen to that."

Then, in a gesture which made Lenny and Jason laugh, Peter raised his hand to speak. Still laughing, Lenny nodded toward the big blond.

"Listen," Peter began in a shaky voice, "we'll make it up to you. I mean, about the gram. I swear it. Just let us get out of here."

Lenny leaned against the Pontiac and pulled out a cigarette and lit it. "I don't know, brother; you dudes almost killed me last night. Wasn't even a fair fight. I mean, I let you fly and what happens next? You bring the whole fucking football team after me or what?"

"No, I promise! No more!" Peter was trembling now, his hands fluttering almost wildly at his sides.

Lenny nodded to Jason, who stepped forward and leveled his pistol at a space between the two white men. A flick of the wrist and he would be able to target either one and fire. Lenny then stepped around the rear of the car, handing his gun to Jason. He walked up to Don, who towered over him, and smiled up into his face.

"Like last night," he said menacingly, "it's two to one. Only you make one move, and my partner'll blow you apart. You dig where I'm coming from?"

Don nodded. His face was frozen into a look of desperation. His blue eyes were washed and unblinking.

Quickly, without warning, Lenny took one step backward, then threw a roundhouse right into Don's lower belly. Don collapsed, half his body falling over from the waist down. He held his stomach with his arms crossed and looked up at Lenny, his eyes pained.

Lenny hit him again with his open hand across the face, spinning the big man to the concrete. This was where he wanted him, directly beneath his feet. "Okay, motherfucker," Lenny breathed as he placed the heel of his boot directly on Don's groin. The big kid lay on the concrete, shaking his head wildly back and forth, silently begging Lenny to stop.

Lenny had used this tactic many times on the streets. He knew he could exert a certain amount of pressure without permanently maiming his opponent—but the immediate results were frightening. Vomiting a horrible mixture of blood and black spittle, and, of course, the incredible pain. The damage would prevent Don from playing around for a couple of weeks, but after that, he would be fine. Lenny enjoyed the thought that he would scare the poor devil to death.

"You didn't have the balls last night," Lenny began

as he pushed down on the man's groin, "to do it all the way. I do. You going to be alive, man, but barely. I mean, you don't have to worry none about women anymore. 'Bout the only thing you be capable of doing is eating a little now and then. You dig?"

Don was shaking his head wildly. He tried to scream, but no sound was produced. Peter stood by and watched, and suddenly he grabbed his stomach and leaned over. He vomited wildly on the concrete, splattering Lenny's leg and Don's face with the vile stuff.

"Jesus shit," Lenny protested. "You dudes just can't control it, can you?"

Don was in horrible pain now, and the fear was mounting. A dark stain appeared at the front of his Levis, and the vile stench of a bowel movement filled the air. Combined with Peter vomiting the scene inside the garage was becoming ugly.

"Man," Jason complained, "I need me a drink. This place stinks."

Lenny chuckled. "One more sec, bro and I'll have this former ladies' man all ready for the fucking church choir!"

Lenny dug his heel in a little deeper and twisted. Don blackened, the color fading completely from his face. He threw his head to the side and began vomiting. The stuff poured out of him slowly and without energy.

"Okay, my man, let's split." Lenny said, removing his heel and picking up the cocaine and pills from the trunk of the car.

Before leaving, Lenny stopped next to the prone, twisted body of Don. He leaned down next to the man's face, resting on his haunches. "Now you remember one thing, asshole," he began in a soft voice. "Next time I meet up with you it's going to be simple. Your fucking brains going to leave your body. You dig where I'm coming from?"

Don, curled up now in the fetus position with his knees tucked under his chin, nodded.

Peter sat five feet away, having dropped to his knees as all his energy and his will left him. He looked like a rag doll that had been dropped from above and had happened to land in that position. He swayed back and forth slowly.

"That man ready for the institution," Lenny commented as he and Jason walked quickly away from the scene.

"Them boys try and play street games," Jason said, "without the tools. Kinda got to feel sorry for them and their lack of brains."

Lenny chuckled sardonically. "Yeah, real sorry . . . until they put two of those motherfucking clowns against one of you. Then, suddenly, you don't feel so bad no more."

Jason threw his arm around his friend as they moved up the stairs and back into the complex.

Lenny poured the whiskey while Jason lay out a couple of lines of the cocaine. Both men were in good spirits after retrieving their stash. But as Lenny placed the tumbler of whiskey on the kitchen table, he frowned.

"Take some of this shit, Lenny," Jason offered, sliding the mirror with the coke on it across the table.

Lenny picked up the straw, leaned over and snorted the white powder into his nose. He finished up two full lines and passed the mirror back to Jason.

"We got to talk, brother," Lenny said in a solemn voice.

Jason finished off the coke and leaned back in his

chair, taking a long sip of the whiskey. "Okay, my man, let it roll."

Lenny sat down and leaned forward, cupping his hands in front of him. "Things ain't as light as we thought they'd be, my man," he began. "Trouble has started coming down around here, and I got me a strange feeling it's gonna get a lot worse before it gets better. Those dudes tonight, I'm sure they'll try something else. Maybe even come after us with a gang of white lames. And my thing with Wanda . . . well, the broad is so hot she's reached the danger level."

Jason threw up his hands. "We just can't walk out on all this. Not with the pussy, the parties . . . man, we in some kind of paradise. A man got to fight for his heaven."

"I dig where you're coming from, bro. But you're hip to what I'm saying as much as me. I'm not sayin' we split at the moment, I'm just sayin' we make sure we take advantage of our situation as much as possible. You dig?"

Jason looked at his friend questioningly.

"Okay," Lenny began in the way of an answer. "Let's take you and the old broad, Sylvia, for instance. I mean, she already lay a couple of bills on you, right?"

Jason nodded, a sheepish grin on his face.

"Okay, but that's peanuts. I mean, if we put some kind of time limit on ourselves, know that we goin' to boogie on out of here, then why not try and hit the broad up for a little more?"

"And you with Wanda? Same shit?"

"Uh huh," Lenny said, his voice softening. "She goin' to flip on me one time or another. And when she does, my ass be in the frying pan, no doubt. She's fallen too hard for a little cock, and it's been too long since she had a man to love her. It can turn a woman around."

131

"Okay," Jason began. "So we hustle the two ladies, don't bother me none. Then what?"

"Well, after we get our financial situation lined up nice and comfortable, we make plans. Maybe head north into L.A., check out the streets there and see what's playin'. If we got ourselves a stake, ain't no reason we can't score real big out here."

"I can dig it," Jason said.

"One more thing," Lenny added. "Old Thadius . . . the old man kind of in deep trouble, being the only brother here and havin' to brown nose everybody in sight. I got me a way to help him out, make sure he gets a piece of these rich white folks pie, too."

Jason laughed. "Thadius? He couldn't handle nothing!"

Lenny got to his feet, checked his watch and grinned. "You just come on down with me and I'll show you how it's done. We'll fix it up real nice."

It was nearing two o'clock when Lenny and Jason finally found the admiral. As usual, the distinguished old man was walking his poodle, and crawling amongst the bushes looking for a good window to peek into. Lenny and Jason found him beneath an open bedroom window, panting as he stared in at a young blonde sitting at her dresser combing her hair. It must have been a good night for the admiral, because the pretty young girl was naked.

"Now, you just follow my lead," Lenny whispered to his partner.

Slowly, the two men moved out of the bushes, across the walkway and directly behind the admiral. They waited for a moment, also taken with the sight of the young nude. Finally, Lenny cleared his throat. The admiral jumped a foot off the ground, spun around on his heels and stood face to face with the two black men. His face was crimson, and his lips moved comically without saying anything.

"Uh . . . I . . . the dog . . . walking the dog . . . ."

Lenny chuckled. "Ain't no reason to be uncool, Admiral. That's one pretty fine young lady sitting there all naked."

The admiral tried to smile, then glanced back over his shoulder at the window. Apparently, the girl had heard the commotion outside, put on a dressing gown and came to the window. She peered out into the darkness.

"What the fuck?" she said.

"Good evening," Lenny chimed.

"Are you guys peeping into my window?" Her voice was irate. "I'll call the police!"

The admiral was quickly falling into a state of collapse. He started mumbling something about his dog, but stopped when Lenny raised his hand.

"Listen, little sister, man here got a lot to lose if you go and call the fuzz. Maybe I can lay something on you what might convince you otherwise."

The girl cocked her head. "What're you talking about?" she asked with interest.

Lenny reached into his pocket and pulled out a vial filled with cocaine. "The best stuff you ever want to snort, honey. Pure as my black skin."

The girl smiled. "Wait a second," she said, turning to her dresser and pulling out a small cocaine kit. Lenny glanced at Jason and smiled. The girl returned to the window, opened the screen and held out her hand. "Lemme try some," she said simply.

Lenny handed her the vial. With an expert's hand she dipped the spoon into the white powder and snorted a hefty amount into her nostril. Then, she repeated the process with the other nostril. She waited for a few moments, then flashed a wide grin. "It's a deal," she said happily.

"That's my mama," Lenny said cheerfully. "An' listen, baby. Anytime you want a little party, you'll meet my partner here and myself at the Jacuzzi."

The girl smiled. "You got it, man." she said.

Lenny reached out and took the admiral's arm, leading him away from the window and down the darkened path. "Man, it could have all been over," Lenny said ominously.

"I'm so ashamed," the admiral blurted.

"Ain't no reason for that," Lenny laughed. "Some of the greatest men in history got off on looking. Powerful men like yourself find it a release from tensions, dig?"

"I . . . I find it that way often. Yes."

" 'Course you do, my man. But the problem is, you in a precarious position. Dig? I mean, an admiral like yourself, you got a lot to lose should something bad come down, like it almost did back there."

"You're absolutely right about that," the admiral agreed.

"Now, it would be a sincere drag if you had to give up on your one pleasure in life. Right?"

"Yes, it would," the admiral replied.

"Well, me and my partner here can fix the whole thing for you . . . sort of like we did back there. You dig where I'm coming from?" Lenny stopped the man in the middle of the path and looked him straight in the eye. "Two yards per month and you safe as a baby in mother's belly."

"Two yards?"

"Yeah," Lenny replied, chuckling. "Two hundred dollars."

The admiral looked from Lenny to Jason. "I don't know . . . ."

Lenny slapped his arm around the man's shoulder. "Man, as far as I can see, you ain't got any choice in the matter. The way things going down around here, it seem like you eventually goin' to get yourself caught. And that would mean newspapers, and all the folks who live here would know about you."

"But two hundred a month?"

"Oh man," Lenny said in exasperation, "you don't know nothing about nothing, do you? I mean, we offering our services to keep you protected, man. To keep you happy and safe in your little hobby. Shit man, if we was your enemies, you'd be in knee deep shit by now, no doubt."

"Well, I thank you for that back there, but . . . ."

"But nothing, man. You think me and my partner in this for profit? Man, that's an insult! We just trying to protect one of America's warriors, helping out where we can. We need that bread for operating money."

The admiral remained silent.

Lenny moved in quickly. "Now, there's a light stand next to building F. I want the money, in a waterproof packet, lying in the tall grass at one o'clock in the morning, every month on the month. Starting tonight."

The admiral nodded helplessly.

"And you can be sure that your little game will continue for as long as you can dig it!"

Lenny took the man's hand and shook it. "C'mon Jason, we got work to do for the admiral." The two black men turned and walked back down the path. The admiral watched them helplessly, then leaned down and scooped his tiny poodle into his arms. He petted the animal delicately, and moaned softly to himself.

CHAPTER TEN

WANDA SET THE RECEIVER back onto the cradle and leaned back in her chair. Around her, the other girls were busy with their morning work, speaking cheerfully with one another about the upcoming weekend. Wanda watched them, thinking about the phone call she had just received from Lenny. His voice had been edgy, he had spoken quickly and directly.

"I need you, babe," he had said. "Right now!"

Wanda had protested that it was still early in the morning, that she had to work to take care of. But

Lenny had not let go. He had insisted that she come up to his apartment that instant. And contrary to her own professional attitudes, Wanda had felt herself loosen against his pleas. That same shaky feeling riddled her body, her legs grew weak and her heart began pumping loudly against her chest. The final blow was the moisture between her legs, an unknown reaction to the highly disciplined woman until she had met Lenny. It was bothering her now that she would react in such a manner.

"Everything alright, Wanda?" the young girl at the reception desk asked.

Wanda nodded, tried to pull herself together as best as possible, and stood up behind her desk. "I think I'm coming down with something. I'd better take a little walk."

The girl smiled and turned back to her desk.

Wanda walked stiffly from the office, into the courtyard, and toward building E. Her head was spinning, and all she could think about was Lenny inside her, his massive cock penetrating her deeply and fully. She climbed the two flights of stairs with trembling steps and paused when she reached the top.

Suddenly, the words which Harold had spoken only that morning came to her. He had called in a highly professional manner, acting almost as her counsel instead of a jilted boyfriend. He had advised her to stay away from the "Negro" on the grounds that a young man like that could be after only one thing, money. Harold , as was his custom, did not ever allow romance or sexuality to enter into a picture, which probably explained why he was still poor as a lawyer. Instead, everything he spoke of was based on certain laws, normal routines of an upper class white society. A young black man, therefore, could not be in love with a white woman older than himself. It was impossible. The only motivation for his attentions, Harold had explained, was Wanda's money. Basically, Harold had summed up, the relationship was a hustle and nothing more.

The words had hurt the woman deeply. Lenny had asked for nothing, except to have the two thugs evicted from the complex. And that had been fine with Wanda. That kind of trouble she did not want, and she was sure the Morris people didn't either. It had been the professional way to end what could have been an explosive situation. And that had been all Lenny had asked for. No money. Harold's suggestion seemed far removed from reality, yet it plagued her just the same.

She walked slowly to the apartment door and knocked lightly. Like in a dream, she was powerless to control her own actions when it came to the young black man.

The door swung open and Lenny stood there with a wide grin on his face and not much else. Wanda was momentarily shocked by his nudity, but the sight of his well-proportioned body only served to heighten the erotic feelings which had invaded her senses since his phone call.

"Hi baby," Lenny said cooly as he stepped aside and allowed her entrance.

He took her quickly into his arms and pressed himself against her. His penis became instantly erect, and Wanda's hand slid down the front of his body to grasp it. She moaned as her fingers closed around the hot shaft.

"Get undressed, babe," Lenny said, standing back and starting to pull off her sweater. Wanda helped him with trembling hands. When she was nude, Lenny kissed her again. Then he placed his hands gently on her shoulders and pushed her down to her knees. Wanda obliged, kissing his black flesh as she traveled the distance to his groin. She held his penis outward and kissed the tip, then parted her lips and took him deep inside her mouth.

"It ain't never been better," Lenny moaned as Wanda moved back and forth on him. "I love you, Wanda," he added.

She responded with a deeper, stronger pull. Then she pulled away and stood up. "Fuck me, baby . . . please!"

Lenny took her hand and led her into the bedroom. He had cocaine ready on the nightstand next to the bed, and gave Wanda some before he started. Then he rubbed some of the powder on his cock and snorted two lines. She lay on the bed, spread-eagled and waiting. Lenny hovered above her, knowing that this would be the fuck of her life.

An hour later, Wanda was sobbing hysterically. Sex with Lenny had never been better. She had reached the heights of her own sexual experience, only to be dropped like a sack of flour to the depths of despair. During the come down period, Lenny had asked her for money, twenty thousand dollars to be exact. And now, she was reacting almost violently. The words of Harold rang through her brain like a taunting nightmare.

"Come on, baby, ain't no big thing," Lenny said evenly, wiping away the tears from her cheeks.

"Oh God!" Wanda half screamed. "Harold warned me!"

"Harold, my ass!" Lenny said, angry now. "Harold little white boy whose daddy gave him everything a man could ever want. Only Harold can't never make it. I was born black, baby, without nothin'! I need money to start a business, to get myself off the ground so you and me can stay together. Otherwise, I got to get myself out of here and hustle the streets. See, my daddy didn't buy me no law degree like Harold's."

Wanda twisted her head back and forth as though in the throes of some kind of perverted ecstasy. She kept repeating the word "no" in a frantic, desperate voice.

Lenny tried another tact. He began kissing her large white breasts, then sliding down to her belly and below. Wanda thrust her hips high off the bed when his tongue invaded her private valley. She squirmed out from beneath him and rolled to the floor.

"Goddammit, you just leave me alone!" she screamed.

"Now come on, baby. Ain't that bad, is it?"

"You bastard! You bastard!"

Lenny shrugged easily and got off the bed. He walked to the dresser, opened the top drawer and pulled out a white envelope. After casually lighting a cigarette, he sat down on the edge of the bed above where Wanda lay on the floor.

"Now listen, honey, once more I ask you. I dig you and all that shit, but times are rough for a nigger like me. I need help, and you're in a position to give it to me. Dig?"

"I won't give you a nickel!" Wanda screamed. "Not a goddamned nickel!"

Lenny chuckled softly as he opened the envelope. "I hate to do this to our sacred love, baby," he said with a sardonic ring in his voice, "but you don't leave me no choice."

He turned the envelope upside down and let the Polaroid snapshots fall to the floor. Wanda sat up slowly and began looking at each one. At first, her eyes darted back and forth across them all, then she began picking them up individually and studying them. Recognition dawned slowly on her.

"This is me," she said softly.

"That's right, mama. And I wouldn't think about destroying them pictures. There's another set in a safe place."

"These are me!" Wanda repeated, this time in a louder voice. It was as if the shock of seeing herself in a sexual role was too much for her, something alien and beyond her imagination. She had never even posed before, and, unlike many young women, had never felt the narcissistic excitement that comes from posing nude for a boyfriend or lover.

And now here she was in print, lying naked and spread-eagled so that every part of her anatomy was clearly visible. In another shot, she had Lenny's penis in her mouth. It was horrible and exciting at the same time, and Wanda was becoming dizzy with the power of its impact.

"Kinda nice shots," Lenny mused, smoking his cigarette. "Think those folks at Morris might enjoy seeing some of them pictures. Not to mention Harold, of course. He might dig the shit out of 'em. Might even get himself a good hardon. Hard to say, though. Man like that might take it all the wrong way. You know?"

Wanda stared up at the smooth black face. Her brow furrowed and her eyes were questioning. It was like staring into the face of an alien now, an entity which she had thought she had known but now realized that she hadn't. She was looking at this tough young black for the first time. He was no longer an ebony-skinned warrior, a gallant and brave native in a strange land. He was no longer the supreme innocent, the crude but happy-go-lucky black man from the streets of New York. As Wanda looked at him, she realized that he was a mean, street-wise punk, a true black bastard.

She came at him with nails and teeth. Lenny laughed

as he grabbed her arms and threw her down onto the bed.

"Listen, babe, you're a nice lady. But you got one problem. You're white and you think like a white. No white ever could get you into this mess. You wouldn't have let it happen. But you did let it come down with a black man. That 'cause you think a black man can't do nothing more than fuck. You like all whiteys, always looking at the color, can't ever get past the damned color. Well, it'll cost you this time, Wanda, but maybe you learnin' the most valuable lesson of your life!"

Wanda struggled free and turned her head toward the window. What had just been spoken to her made a strange kind of sense. The words had hit her hard, and she realized that, for the most part, Lenny was right.

"I'll get the money," she said quietly.

Lenny turned away from her and poured out some of the cocaine onto the nightstand. Without using a razor blade to grade it fine, he leaned over with the straw and snorted a huge amount into his nostril.

"Was it like this from the beginning?" Wanda asked after a long silence.

Lenny shook his head. "Uh uh. But things are going down and turning around, and there's things me and Jason got to do." His voice was almost apologetic. "I saw the situation between you and Harold, and I knew nothin' would ever happen between us. You got your head wrapped so tightly you can't hardly breathe no more. But that's the way white man's world work."

Wanda nodded. "It would be too far for me to go to free myself of all that, wouldn't it?"

Lenny nodded. "Most white people go crazy when they hit the streets. The world's too real out there. White folks live like they're on television or something. Like this apartment house, one big television show. And it ain't even that good."

Wanda laughed at the analogy.

Lenny looked down at her and smiled. "You want some more coke?"

"Why not?" Wanda sighed.

Lenny fixed up another couple of lines. After she had finished he began stroking her hair gently.

"You know something funny," Wanda said.

Lenny waited for her to speak.

"Those pictures . . . I actually got a little thrill out of seeing myself like that."

"It ain't funny, babe, it's normal. Everybody wants to be sexy. Turning on the world is what it's all about."

He leaned down and kissed her, and she responded with a healthy surge. Lenny began chuckling, and Wanda pulled away quickly.

"What's so funny?" she asked.

"This is the damndest blackmail I ever seen!" Lenny laughed.

And Wanda began laughing also. She continued giggling and stopped only when Lenny kissed her again.

Thadius hopped from one foot to the other, a big smile etched on his face. In his hand he held a waterproof envelope.

"Goddamn, brother, it was there just like you said!"

Lenny and Jason both laughed. "We told you, my man," Lenny said easily. "A cakewalk."

Suddenly the smile disappeared from the old man's face. He looked wearily out the window to the courtyard below. "But what happens, man, when you guys split?"

Lenny held up his hand. "Man, we got this dude nailed to the wall. Ain't no way he going to question nothing. He's got everything in the world to lose and nothing to gain by coming down on us. Besides, he don't even know you're involved. He just think 'cause he drop that money there every month he in fine shape. Honkie lames all think like that."

Thadius shook his head and smiled. "Man can have some fun with this bread, do a little jiving around town 'fore I go to my grave!"

"That's the way we work, Thadius," Jason added. "Dude treat us right, we do all right by him. And you're gonna hear a lot more 'bout that style soon as me and Lenny get ourselves set up."

"Hey!" Thadius shouted, not listening to Jason. "That dude looking for you? First round after the game is on me."

Lenny looked quickly to Jason, then back to Thadius. "What dude, Thadius?" he asked evenly.

"Why the ex-football player. Man who played with O.J.? Wandering around here in the dead of night looking for you cats. Seems he lost his baggage at the airport or something and couldn't remember your apartment number. He said we all going to the Rams scrimmage on Saturday."

Lenny slapped his leg with a little too much enthusiasm. "Shit man, that must be Leroy!"

Thadius nodded eagerly. "Man didn't say what his name was. Forgot to ask, too much rapping about his days with the Juice up at 'Frisco State to worry about names."

"Yeah, goddamn," Lenny began again. "Old Leroy! Must have found himself some good pussy on the way up to the pad, forgot all about his good old friends."

"Little pussy make a man do that real easy," Jason nodded. "By the way, Thadius, he still big like always?"

"Don't know nothing about always," Thadius replied. "But he was one big sucker. Face looked as though he stopped a battleship with it."

"That's old Leroy!" Lenny laughed. "Ugly as they come, but the women really go for him. Must be the size of his hands or something."

The three men laughed, and Lenny jumped to his feet and adroitly moved Thadius out of the apartment. "You do well with that bread, old friend," Lenny said as he virtually pushed the little guard out into the hallway.

"Sure will man, and appreciate every cent of it." Thadius beamed as the door closed in his face.

Lenny turned back to Jason. Both men were serious.

"Churchman," Lenny said.

Jason nodded. "Sounds like him. How the fuck did he find us?"

Lenny shook his head. "The fucking car," he snapped. "Must have been the fucking car!"

Jason lit a cigarette and took a long drag. "You think Hodding sent him?"

" 'Course he did," Lenny replied. "Churchman the only street mechanic who knows us. Besides, he probably came cheap. Man too ugly to do anything else in this life."

"Shit man," Jason complained "I didn't think Hodding would try for us out here, not on account of what happened back there."

Lenny poured a drink and sipped slowly on the whiskey. "Man, you fool with another man's woman, that's bad. But when you fool with a white woman that belong to a powerful nigger, that's deadly. Hodding had a lot of green cash invested in that babe, and I just ambled in real cool like and snatched up that white pussy. Make a man mad."

"What we gonna do, Lenny?" Jason said.

Lenny walked to the window and looked down at the tanned bodies ringing the pool. "Well," he began slowly, "we got the edge now 'cause we know he's here. His greatest weapon, the element of surprise, is long gone now."

"You think he'll try and hit us here?" Jason asked.

"Probably not up here," Lenny replied. "Too wide open up here, hard to get down these fucking stairs and out of here. No, he'll probably wait till we get out on the streets. Maybe even try in the garage. That's where I'd take my shots . . . right down there in the garage."

"Man, we can't just sit around here for weeks waiting on him to strike!"

"Nope," Lenny agreed. "We got to pull our shit together. I already got Wanda to the bank this morning. She should be back this evening with a whole wad for us. How'd you make out with Sylvia?"

Jason shook his head. Woman's broke as I am. She ain't got nothing 'cept her social security and a little savings. That two fifty was probably the first and last coin I ever see from that bitch."

"No matter, my man. The twenty thou' from Wanda should be enough to get us off the ground up in L.A. Anyway, this scene down here too fucking lame for my blood. I want some night life, clubs and sounds and foxy brown sisters. I'm getting tired of dried up white pussy."

Jason laughed. "You ain't looked if you been too tired, partner."

Lenny grinned back. "I ain't saying I was *too* tired, just tired. Lames out here get to you after a while."

Jason nodded his agreement. "Okay, then. We split this scene as soon as possible. But meantime, we stay armed, right?"

"That's right, partner. And we don't leave each other's side, neither. I mean, you got to come in and watch me and Wanda, well, that's just part of staying alive here. Dig?"

"You and Wanda. Ain't no big thing . . . ."

Lenny laughed, set down his drink and threw a mock punch at his friend. Jason returned the jab.

"We gonna make it in L.A., brother. Real big!" Lenny laughed as he spoke. But it was obvious to Jason that his partner was worried.

CHAPTER ELEVEN

CHURCHMAN TRUDGED up the flight of stairs to his second floor room. Once inside, he threw himself down upon the bed, exhausted from another night of watching the Palmwood Gardens. Two in a row he had spent wandering in and out of the complex, waiting for any sign from room E-319. He had spotted their rented car already, and knew that the two men rarely, if ever, left their room. He wondered if somehow they had been informed of his presence, and if they were playing cat and mouse with him. It was impossible to tell.

The phone rang, bringing Churchman out of his thoughts. The voice on the other end belonged to Clinton Jones.

"What's up, my man?" Jones asked in a slow speech pattern.

"Nothing," Churchman answered bluntly.

"I've spoken to the man in the Big Apple," Jones began. "He's a little uptight about the lack of action out here on this coast. You dig where I'm coming from?"

Churchman sighed. "Man, it's too dangerous to do the thing in the apartment itself. I got to wait until they show themselves."

Clinton Jones' tone turned from friendliness to anger. "Man ain't paying you ten thousand green ones for an easy job, my man. Man paying you to take a certain amount of risk. You dig where I'm coming from?"

Churchman weighed what Jones was telling him. Obviously, the man in New York, Carter Hodding, was becoming impatient. He had been on the coast now for four days, and the results were negative. Not even a plan. And Carter Hodding was not the kind of man to wait around for any length of time.

"Okay," Churchman said after a lengthy silence. "It'll be done tonight."

"You got a plan?" Jones snapped.

"Somewhat. I'm gonna wait in the garage. If nothing's cooking by midnight, I'll do it in the pad."

"Okay," Jones said, the friendly tone returning to his voice. "Your Caddy running alright?"

"Yeah, fine." Churchman replied.

"Good. I'll arrange a three o'clock flight out of LAX for you. Just drop the car at the agency, everything'll be taken care of. A man will meet you at Kennedy tomorrow."

Churchman hesitated a moment before speaking. "Listen, Jones?" he began.

"Yeah, brother?" came the reply.

"If I don't cut it tonight, there's a little lady staying in my pad on Lexington. I mean, if the job is done but I get wasted, could you make sure the rest of my coin is laid on her?"

"Hey man," Jones cried, "don't talk down like that! No jive shit is going to happen, man. You be in and out of there in two seconds, the deed will be done, the green will flow and New York will be all yours. Dig?"

Churchman chuckled into the receiver. "Yeah. Simple as that, huh?"

"Even simpler," Jones replied. "Now you got the situation straight in your head?"

"Yeah," Churchman sighed. Once again, they were talking down to him, taking him for a fool. He wondered how long it would be in this short life before other men would start regarding him as an equal.

"Okay, my man," Jones said before hanging up. "You be cool, and I'm sure we'll do the scene again."

The other end went dead. Churchman held the receiver out at arm's length and stared at it for a few moments. For some reason, the nagging suspicions still remained. Jones' voice, his exhortations to complete the job fast, everything about him created a sense of distrust in Churchman. But, then again, that was the nature of the world into which he had entered. It was a world of killers—the killed and the killer. Men's lives were bought and sold, and no one trusted anyone else. It was the life that Churchman had been preparing himself for for many years. He could not back out of it now.

Churchman had made a study of some of the most famous street mechanics in New York City, how they spent the hours prior to a hit, how they handled the nerves so that they would be in top form once the moment of truth arrived. One man Churchman knew about spent his time in a cathouse. He would buy three women for a couple of hours, and lounge around with them eating a light meal and drinking just a little wine. According to rumors, he would never actually reach a sexual climax, but would excite himself to the very brink. He claimed that it put himself on the very edge of awareness, heightened his senses without dispelling the energy. Another mechanic whom Churchman knew about went to Central Park and fed pigeons. Did nothing but feed pigeons for the hours before a hit.

Churchman sat on the edge of his bed, thinking about these men and their professional mannerisms. He had not been in the business long enough to know what worked. He would have to move purely on instinct, without tradition.

Churchman spent the better part of the day cleaning his two .38s, making sure that they worked smoothly and efficiently. He applied a little salve to his double shoulder holster to make sure that an easy draw would be possible. Also, he applied some stickum to the bottom of his shoes, knowing that concrete could become slippery, especially in a garage where cars continually leaked oil. A slip could be deadly in his game, and Churchman planned not to slip.

As sunset neared, the large black man left his motel room and strolled out to the bay. He walked slowly along the quiet water, smoking cigarette after cigarette, watching the young boys and girls as they played and strolled along the beachfront. He reached a large restaurant overlooking the harbor and walked inside. Sitting alone at a large booth, he ordered a steak, salad and a beer. He finished his meal with a cup of black coffee.

Back in his motel room, Churchman began making his final moves toward his goal. He took a long, hot shower and dressed himself carefully in his best clothes. Before leaving the room, he made himself a cup of instant coffee and downed two small amphetamine tablets.

With suitcase in hand, Churchman walked to his Cadillac, got in and started the short drive across the bridge to the Palmwood Gardens apartment complex.

There was a parking space just across the street from

the entrance to the parking lot itself. Churchman pulled into the spot and turned off the engine. He waited for a few moments inside the car, mentally planning his escape route. If the hit took place in the apartment, he would run across the courtyard, down into the garage and out the entrance to his car across the street. If it took place in the garage itself, the escape would be easier and consume less time. It would be a matter of crossing the street and nothing more. Churchman prayed silently to himself that the hit would be made in the garage. He knew he had a time limit, Jones had imposed that already. And midnight was his deadline. If nothing happened by then, he would have to enter the building and make the hit inside the apartment—a risk that he did not want to take.

The night air was cool, a soft wind had risen off the ocean to the west. Churchman locked his car door, checked his weapons in his holster, and moved casually across the street and into the garage. The underground cavern was empty of life. Churchman moved quickly toward the rented Chevrolet parked in the middle of the row. He breathed a little easier seeing the car. His worst fear that Lenny and Jason had left during his absence was not realized. So far, he was on target.

Parked directly in front of the Chevrolet, and facing the entrance to the lot from the courtyard, was a large pick-up truck. It was a perfect hiding place. The height of the cab would allow Churchman to stand, and thus view all the entrances to the lot. And the bulk of the vehicle itself would give him time to hide if he saw anyone approaching.

Churchman reached for a cigarette and lit it quickly. Suddenly, his nerves quieted and his mind became very clear. The speed was working its magic on his system, and his job was defined in a clear perspective. No more waiting. As the sun rose in the east he would be on a plane heading into New York City—a rich man by his standards and a man with a future.

Churchman checked his watch. It was now eight-thirty. Three and a half hours would tell the story. With the cold resignation of a professional, he settled in for the wait.

Don sat at the long table picking at the huge meal before him. The garish light of the dining room seemed to lessen the glow of his tan. He looked peaked and almost frail.

His mother watched him closely as he ate. She hadn't seen her only son for nearly a month, and she sensed that something was definitely wrong. Coming home like he had the night before, tired and apparently hurt, had shocked both her and Don's father. Yet the boy had been reclusive about his activities, just asking for his old room back and quietly going to sleep.

Now, he sat at the table without saying a word. His father, a tall slim man with silver hair and the air of wealth about him, sipped his wine slowly and watched his son. Finally, he broke the silence. "You want to tell us about it, son?" Don's father said in a low, even voice. The man was an executive with Boeing, and never lost his corporate demeanor.

"Nothing to tell, Dad," Don said simply.

Don's father looked to his mother. She lowered her eyes, not knowing whether or not to participate.

"Something's wrong, son," he continued. "Your mother and I can see that much."

For a brief moment, Don looked to his parents like a small child, a child who somehow had found himself in deep trouble and needed his parents desperately. There was even the hint of a tear in his eye. But as quickly as that look appeared, it vanished. It was replaced by the normal, arrogant posture of a young man born into wealth and security.

Don's father shrugged his shoulders and returned to his meal.

"I've got to go now," Don said suddenly.

"I have dessert, honey," his mother said.

Don rose from the table. "No thank you. Peter and I are meeting with some people tonight. I don't have time."

He left the table quickly. His parents watched him exit the room and then returned to their silent meal.

Don grabbed his leather jacket from his old closet, and dashed outside to his Pontiac. His groin still hurt terribly, but Don was used to injuries and the pain they caused. After six years of high school and junior college football, he had learned to live with almost any kind of pain.

Peter was waiting in the garage behind his parents' luxurious home in the Corona Del Mar area south of Newport Beach. The front house was dark and empty. Every year, Peter's parents took a three month cruise to some new port of interest. Peter was also the only child of a millionaire.

"Is everything ready?" Don asked in a very serious voice.

Peter nodded, turned on the overhead light and gestured to the workbench behind him. Spread out as though for sale were three .22 pistols, with shells lined up neatly next to them. "Dad's got the magnum in a bank vault, I couldn't get to it."

"Shit," Don said. "These .22s are hardly worth firing. I mean, you can shoot a man ten times with one of these and never kill him."

Peter grinned. "It depends on where you hit him, Don. It depends on where you hit him."

Peter picked up one of the pistols and fired the pin a couple of times as if to demonstrate. "Got to go for the face," he said in a cold voice. "Got to go for the face."

Don nodded. "Let's get these things loaded and get over there. We might have to wait inside that garage for a fucking long time."

Ceremoniously, they loaded the pistols. Don took two of the guns and put one each in the pockets of his leather coat. Peter stuffed his gun down the front of his pants. They shut off the light in the garage and climbed into the Pontiac. Before starting the engine, Don turned to his partner. "You got any more quaaludes?"

"Outasight," Peter grinned, pulling out a small tin filled with the pills. He gave two to Don and popped two into his own mouth.

"This should put us just right," Don said as he backed out of the driveway.

They took the coast highway out of Corona and toward Balboa. Don drove very slowly, almost with ceremony, through the sparse traffic.

"You know," he began, his voice beginning to show the effects of the tranquilizers, "I never really knew any niggers until those two. My dad used to talk about them all the time, saying how they were populating faster than the white man in America so they could take it over."

Peter nodded slowly. "They do that so they can get more welfare. It's part of the game."

Don agreed. "My dad told me once that niggers are like animals, that they don't have consciences like we do. Instead, they just go along with whatever comes in front of them. Like, they don't have a general perspective about anything."

"Well," Peter drawled, "those two at the Gardens sure proved that! I mean, walking in there and fucking white girls and ripping people off. I mean, who the hell did they think they were, anyway!"

"That's what I mean about sense. They don't have any. They don't care. I guess they'd just as soon go back to the jungle."

Peter laughed and imitated a baboon scratching himself. Don joined in, but stopped suddenly.

"What's happening, man?"

"Look over there!" Don said, pointing across the street to two young girls standing on the corner with their thumbs out.

"Hey man, we can't stop," Peter said. "We got to get down there and wait this thing out."

Don laughed. "Oh man, those fucking niggers don't expect trouble. They think were running scared now. Last thing in the world they'll think is that we're out gunning for them."

Don slowed the car down and pulled to the curb. The two girls, both very young and very blonde, smiled. "We got to be as relaxed as possible," Don grinned. "That's the way real hit men do it."

Peter shrugged and opened the car door. The two girls giggled and crawled into the space between Peter and Don.

"You ladies want some quaaludes?" Don asked as he pulled away from the curb.

Both girls nodded eagerly. "You guys out for some fun?" the one sitting next to Don asked.

Don laughed loudly. "A whole lot of fun, baby, like all night long!"

Peter handed the girls their pills, then slapped the dashboard in enthusiasm. "Right on, man! This is going to be one hell of a night!"

Don, instead of staying on the coast road which would have taken him directly to the Palmwood Gardens apartment complex, turned off on a little used access road toward the beach. He knew of a little cove where everyone skinny dipped and where a man with a full wallet could get any kind of high he wanted.

Clinton Jones drove his Continental slowly by the main entrance to the Palmwood Gardens apartment complex, cruised to the end of the block and turned around again. This was the fifth time he had made the same pass.

The slight, nervous black man sitting in the passenger's seat chain smoked the entire time. In his lap he held a leather travel bag securely between his legs. His pock-marked face and thin goatee gave him the appearance of a totally evil man. While some people called him that, he preferred the name "the destroyer." "Because," he like to say, "after all, I ain't in the business of building things, am I?"

Clinton Jones peered into the main entrance of the parking lot, then turned quickly to his right and fixed his gaze on the white Cadillac. It was nine-thirty in the evening, and the traffic was light. According to the plan, Churchman would at this moment be inside the garage, waiting for his targets to emerge.

"Man," the destroyer said as he drove past the entrance one more time, "we goin' do the thing or just cruise all night long?"

The impatience in his voice grated on Jones' nerves. "You think I'm some kinda fool? Goddamn man, we sittin' out here in white man's heaven, got to be cool!"

The destroyer sighed and lit another cigarette with the lit tip of the one he was smoking.

"Think it's a good idea to smoke around that stuff?" Jones asked, looking down at the satchel.

"Shit man, show what you know! Stuff in here ain't dynamite like in them cowboy movies. This shit is fine plastic! Got to send an electrical charge through it, my man. That's why it so good in cars. Works real nice with the ignition system."

Clinton Jones shrugged. The business was a strange one. A telephone call from Carter Hodding only hours after Churchman's arrival, and Hodding had been very direct. He had given Jones the destroyer's name and number, calling him the best in the business. The hit was to be a double, as Hodding had put it. The target and the hit man.

Jones had accepted the order without question. It was not unusual, especially in a hit that involved a personal vendetta, to use a newcomer and then use a pro to eliminate him. Business was always one thing, but personal hits were another. The emotions involved tended to cloud men's perspectives. And often times, the hit man himself would claim a certain power and intimacy with the man who hired him because of the nature of the job. Carter Hodding could stand to have no man that close to him. Lenny, by his actions with Hodding's girlfriend, had made the New York boss vulnerable. Churchman was keeping that vulnerability alive by eliminating the original cause. But Churchman, by proxy, would still carry the "disease." Thus, Churchman would have to go, too.

Clinton Jones pulled to a stop next to the Cadillac. The destroyer whistled his relief. " 'Bout time, my man. Wondered what the shit I was gettin' paid for, anyway!"

"Just move it, man!" Jones ordered.

The destroyer bolted from the car, unlocked the Cadillac's door easily, then raised the hood. Jones watched in the darkness as the slight man pulled a packet from the satchel and placed it on the manifold near the distributor. He fooled with a couple of wires, checked his system over, then closed the hood softly.

"That'll do her, my man," the destroyer said.

Clinton Jones nodded his satisfaction. "Quick," he said in the manner of a compliment.

"And quicker when it goes," the destroyer replied ominously.

Clinton Jones smiled, and raced the car past the apartment complex and onto the coast road. there was a big party in Los Angeles for a new rock group out of Detroit, and Clinton Jones wanted to be there.

CHAPTER TWELVE

IT TOOK WANDA OVER AN HOUR to withdraw twenty thousand dollars in cash. Under normal conditions, the bank would not have allowed the withdrawal without prior notice, but since Wanda kept a round figure of forty thousand in her account, she was treated as a very important customer. She asked for the money in small bills, and took the huge envelope handed to her by the bank's vice-president and stuffed it gingerly into her purse.

"You be careful," he had said.

Wanda had smiled nervously. "I'll try."

As she drove back to her Newport apartment to change, she thought about the squeeze that had been put on her by Lenny. Blackmail under these conditions had produced the strangest combination of excitement and anger she had ever known. Possibly, it was the sheer boredom of her existence which had allowed her to enjoy this interlude. She didn't know, and she didn't care. All she knew was that even though she was being taken for a huge sum of money, she was enjoying it.

Harold stood outside her apartment door, hands folded across his chest, chubby fingers holding a cigarette. He looked angry in a pouting sort of way. "Hello Wanda," he said coldly.

Wanda nervously tried to get the key into the lock. The last person she wanted to see on this night was Harold. Especially since she was carrying twenty thousand dollars around in her purse.

"Harold, I can't see you now. You'd better go."

Harold threw his cigarette to the carpet and ground it out slowly. It was an exaggerated effort, one that looked like it had been lifted from the movies. His tough guy act made Wanda laugh.

"Come on, Harold," Wanda said bitterly. "Go call your mother or something, she'll make everything alright. Maybe you could borrow some more money from them and go to Tijuana for the night."

Wanda stepped into her apartment, knowing that if Harold followed her, the barrage would continue. Without a word, he did follow.

"What are you doing here, Harold?" Wanda asked finally.

"I just wanted to see you, Wanda," his voice was cold, but at the same time filled with that cracking sense of self-pity which Wanda had heard so many times before.

Wanda shook her head. "Jesus Christ, little man," she began in a strained voice. "Haven't you done enough damage already! By God, Harold, I'm not going to play your mother for you. You can't even get it up for me anymore, why the hell should I bother?"

"You've changed, Wanda," Harold said weakly. "Ever since that nigger came along. What's happened between us?"

Wanda laughed sardonically. "The only thing we ever had was your love of suffering, Harold. And don't call Lenny a 'nigger,' he's got more man in one inch of his cock that you'll ever hope to have!"

Harold was shocked. His face turned even paler, and the flabby skin around his jowls began to pulsate with anger. He raised his arm over his head, let his hand dangle for a moment, then brought it down in a sweeping arc toward Wanda's face.

The blow struck Wanda dead on the cheek, and she went flying backward and onto the carpet. Like most men who never use their bodies, Harold was much stronger than he knew. Even though he had never worked at developing himself, those muscles still went through a maturation process. And, unlike an athletic person, the use of those muscles was a special moment and called for deeper concentration, thus more strength.

Wanda lay on the floor, frightened. The blow had felt as though it had shattered her jaw. Her head was spinning, and the room was difficult to bring back into focus. "Go away, Harold!" she finally managed to say.

But Harold was angry. "Goddamn nigger!" he whined as he took a step closer to the woman. He brought his foot back and almost daintily swung it out in the direction of Wanda's midsection. The toe hit her between the ribs and forced a cry from her throat.

"Please, Harold . . . no more!"

"I'm gonna kill all of you," Harold screamed, his voice rising like a woman's. "I'm gonna kill you, then that nigger. You're animals! Dirty, rotten animals!"

He dropped to his knees with a thud, reached out and yanked Wanda to a sitting position by pulling on her hair. Still holding her with his left hand, he began slapping her face with the right, over and over again until a stream of blood appeared pouring out of her nostril.

Wanda felt powerless beneath the madness which Harold now showed. She knew that she was dealing with a psychotic personality, and that there was no way she could stop him. She hoped that he would run out of steam before he killed her.

The blows were dealt continuously, almost like a child would as he slammed his fist against his pillows in anger. Harold's eyes were half closed, and his mouth twisted into a contorted and almost obscene grin. And, as he continued to hit her, he began moaning, rolling his head, which now seemed too large for his body, back and forth.

And then, suddenly, he stopped. His hand dropped limply to his side and sat there panting, sweat pouring down his forehead. He opened his eyes slowly and stared at the frightened woman. Slowly, he got to his feet.

Wanda watched him as he stood above her, unbuckled his pants and pulled them down. He reached inside his shorts and pulled out his weak little prick, showing it to her as though proud of the fact that it had reached a semi-erect state. He grinned down at her obscenely.

"Oh my God!" Wanda cried in a choked sob. She turned away from him and buried her face in the carpet. She felt as though she was going to be sick.

"Nigger ain't got nothing I ain't got!" Harold boasted in an almost silly voice. "I just need . . . a little action, is all. I'm a man . . . of action . . . ."

"Go away, Harold. Get out!" Wanda spoke with her face buried in the carpet, still unable to look at the half naked man who stood above her. In this one moment, he had revealed himself totally, and she had come to the conclusion that he was somewhat retarded. Either that or so demented that his mind had been affected. She wanted him out, desperately wanted him to go to someone else's home and bring his own kind of sadness with him.

"Please Harold, no more. Just get out."

Harold still grasped his penis and smiled obscenely. Slowly, the smile faded and he began adjusting his clothing. Wanda watched him as he turned to leave. His head bowed, his body still, he walked out of the apartment.

Wanda got to her feet slowly. Her face hurt like hell, and her mid-section was throbbing with pain. She made her way into the bathroom and gasped when she saw herself in the mirror. Swelling was already beginning around her eyes and her mouth. Blood was plastered on her upper lip, and portions of her bottom lip were torn open. She began dabbing water on the bruises, and trying to fix herself up as well as possible. She still had to see Lenny tonight.

Lenny and Jason sat in the living room of their apartment, suitcases stacked on the floor, a bottle of Jack Daniels rested on the coffee table in front of them. Lenny leaned over and poured another round of drinks.

"She should've been here by now, partner," Lenny mused as he sipped from the glass.

"She'll show, brother. That lady has got the royal hots for you. Ain't no way she'll bug out now."

Lenny laughed. "Man, I'll be happy to get up to L.A. with some brothers after all this shit down here. I mean, dealing with some hip sisters again going to be nice."

"I'll drink to that, brother," Jason said, raising his glass and toasting the notion.

"I got it all figured, brother," Lenny began slowly. "We get ourselves a fine pad up near the strip, like somewhere near where we got that coke early on. Maybe we find that same connect again, remember?"

"That little faggot? Sure do, my man. Dude's hot enough, got his fire down below. He'll deal straight with us."

"No doubt, my man," Lenny grinned. "I figure with a stake like we goin' to have, we'll score maybe two, three ounces of the shit and get ourselves a good cutter, some dude with procaine. Double our investment right out the gate. We keep moving on that kind of scene, Jason, we bring down six, maybe seven grand a month. A little play money, you dig?"

Jason slapped Lenny's hand and laughed. "And we be dealing with brothers and sisters. No crazies like we find down here."

"Uh uh, no way. White kids playing a different game, my man. They all hung up trying to straighten up their fucking sex lives to play it straight. No, we need us some heavy duty dudes."

Jason turned away from his partner and sipped slowly at his drink. "And what about our main man in the East, Carter Hodding? He goin' to let Churchman return without our bodies?"

"Churchman found us once 'cause we blew it with the wheels. That mistake," Lenny said in a cold voice, "will never be made again. Once we get our asses up into Los Angeles, we disappear. We got enough bread to cover ourselves."

"Okay, my man. Hope what you layin' down works. But first, we got to get the money." Jason checked his watch. It was now ten o'clock. Lenny had told him that Wanda would be over before eight o'clock with the money. She was already two hours late.

165

"Don't get uptight, my man," Lenny laughed, pouring another round of drinks. "Lady will be by."

They waited another half hour, passing the time by discussing their plans for L.A. A knock at the door broke the anxious mood. Lenny moved casually across the room to answer it.

"Hey baby," Lenny said softly as he opened the door. He did not notice the wounds on Wanda's face until she actually entered the apartment. "Jesus shit, babe, what's goin' down?"

Wanda nodded to Jason, then turned to Lenny. "Nothing, Lenny. Don't ask. I've got the money, that's all you should be interested in."

Lenny traced the swollen features of the pretty woman with gentle fingers. "Harold do this to you, babe?"

Wanda shook her head. "The money, Lenny, I've got the money." She reached into her purse and pulled out the stuffed envelope. Lenny took it and threw it on the coffee table.

"I don't give a fucking shit about the money, Wanda. I wanna know who did this to you. Just say the name."

Wanda started to cry. At first, they were gentle tears, but her voice began to choke up and soon she was sobbing like a small child, periodically trying to catch her breath. "Oh Lenny, it was horrible!" she wailed over and over again.

"Then it was Harold!" Lenny shouted.

Wanda nodded affirmatively. "He's crazy, Lenny. Leave him alone, he's crazy."

Lenny mixed her a gin and tonic and sat her down on the couch. He glanced at Jason who was busy counting the money. Jason looked to his friend and nodded as if to say it was all there. Lenny turned back to Wanda.

"Baby," he began in a soft voice, "you done me and

Jason right by this money here. We owe you something, dig? You tell me where the motherfucker lives, and we'll take care of it before we leave for L.A."

Wanda shook her head. "You'll kill him, Lenny. And he's just crazy. He's pitiful. He's not even a man!"

"Bullshit," Lenny screamed. "Dude beat up on you like this, he needs some teaching about the facts of life, you dig. He need to know what comes afterwards! And I plan to show him!"

Wanda choked on her drink and kept muttering the word "no" over and over again.

"Listen babe," Lenny began, "either you tell me where the motherfucker lives, or I sit down here till I find him. Now, at the moment, I just plan to teach him a lesson. But if I have to wait to find him, I'll make sure he never raises that fat arm of his agin. You dig where I'm coming from?"

"You mean you'll kill him?"

Lenny nodded. "Where does he live, Wanda?"

"On the Lido. 212 Palm Avenue." Wanda broke down and began sobbing again. Lenny stroked her hair gently.

Jason nodded to his partner, signaling him to come into the bedroom.

"You crazy, man?" Jason began, anger in his voice. "We got the bread, we got the wheels out of here, and now you want to wander around in some rich man's neighborhood and mess up some no 'count boy!"

Lenny lit a cigarette. "Listen, my man, this lady going to be one of our valuable assets in the future. She's ripe for us, and she got the means to help us along. I mean, look at this place here! She be our contact inside this apartment and we unload shit through her like you wouldn't believe. And we never have to deal with whitey ourselves. Way I got it figured, we could do two, maybe three thousand a month down here without even moving."

Jason shook his head. "It ain't worth it, Lenny. A white man, rich, he lives in a white man's country out here. He'll come after you with everything he got."

Lenny smiled. "Not this white boy, Jason. He's scared shitless of his own shadow. He won't bother coming after nobody no how. I guarantee you that."

Jason was still not convinced. He stopped Lenny from leaving the room by grabbing his arm. "Listen man, you hung up over this white chick?" Jason asked simply.

Lenny looked directly into his partner's eyes. "The lady's got money, Jason. And she's got enough class to know when she's beat. I mean, that woman ever let herself go a little, she going to be something else. She smarter than most men I know, and I think she's on the verge of putting it all together. Yeah, I got the hots for her. But besides that, I know a good investment when I see one. This lady going to help us get our asses in gear all over this beach town. She going to be our connect into the straight world of whitey down here."

"And what's going to happen when she sees you with a sister sometime?"

Lenny chuckled. "Shit man, Wanda knows where it's at. She digs me, but she knows she can't have me. She's gonna ride with that for a long time, brother, don't you worry your black ass about that!"

Jason shook his head and smiled. "Well, she was real with the twenty grand," he admitted.

Lenny rested his hand affectionately on his friend's shoulder. "I know my ladies, Jason. And there's no doubt this one going to help us along the road to sweet success."

Wanda had pulled herself together, and was sipping

at her gin and tonic when Jason and Lenny returned to the living room.

"You better now, babe?" Lenny asked, sitting next to her and taking her hand.

Wanda nodded. "I'm just confused, Lenny," she said softly.

"Don't be," Lenny replied. "Me and Jason take care of everything and we'll be settled in L.A. by morning. I'll phone you here, okay?"

Wanda smiled weakly. "You'll really call?"

Lenny laughed. "Baby, we going to see a whole lot of each other for a long time, don't you doubt that." And then he smiled, a playful, friendly grin. "I like to keep in close touch with those people I blackmail."

Wanda laughed, and kissed him quickly on the cheek.

CHAPTER THIRTEEN

DON STRETCHED OUT ON THE SAND and stared up at the stars over his head. The quaaludes had taken effect, and the sky appeared smooth and soft. The girl resting next to him rested her hand playfully on his exposed cock, tickling him and running her fingers through his pubic hair.

They had driven to the secluded cove, and by the time they had arrived everyone had been stoned. Surprisingly, they had been alone on this warm, clear night. The girls had paired off quickly. The shorter of the two having gone with Peter. Don had taken his girl down the beach and undressed her quickly. She had a firm, young body. Her boyish hips and relatively small breasts were exciting. As soon as she was naked, she had run into the surf, calling for Don to join her. He had stripped quickly, and followd her into the warm waters. She had come after him instantly, her hands going for his sex as the waves moved their bodies against one another. They had run, hand in hand, back onto the sand. Don had taken her quickly and without much foreplay. It hadn't been the first time it had happened like this. The beaches seemed to release the inhibitions of the girls who lived there.

"What're you thinking?" the girl asked as she kissed Don's belly.

"Nothin," Don replied sharply. "Me and Peter got to go."

"Oh really?" she asked. "Are you sure about that?"

She smiled as she moved lower down his belly. Her lips encircled his cock, but Don pushed her away.

"Jesus," she cried. "You didn't have to do that!"

"Shut up!" Don bellowed, as he staggered to his feet. For a moment he was dizzy and he fell back to the sand. The girl laughed.

"You really handle your dope well," she said bitterly, angered by his rejection.

Don ignored her and struggled to pull on his Levis and the rest of his clothing. When he was dressed, he called out after Peter. From a few yard down the beach, he heard his friend's laughing voice. Don walked uneasily toward the source, and found Peter sitting naked next to his friend. She was lying sprawled on the sand, totally nude, and made no effort to cover herself when Don and his girl approached.

"C'mon Peter, we've got something to do."

Peter giggled, and stroked himself obscenely. "Yeah, I know," he laughed.

Don grabbed his friend's shoulder and squeezed hard. "C'mon man, we ain't got much time!"

Peter grinned idiotically up at Don. "Far out . . ." he moaned. He turned to the nude girl next to him and stroked her pubis. "I got to go, man. Me and Don got to kill some people."

The girl laughed. "Okay, man, whatever's fair."

Peter dressed slowly, and finally stood up next to Don.

"C'mon," Don said to the girls. "Get dressed."

Both girls giggled. "Uh uh. You guys either stay here with us, or go. But we're not leaving. We're just going to stay out here naked until some real men come along!" Both girls broke out into insane laughter and hugged one another.

"Okay, fuck 'em," Don said angrily, grabbing Peter's arm and leading him across the sand toward the Pontiac.

"You sure we ought to leave them out there?" Peter asked. "They're pretty fucked up."

"Forget 'em, man," Don said. "They get raped, that's their problem, not ours."

The lights of the coast highway played havoc with Don's vision. He tried to concentrate on the center line of the highway, but he was virtually lost in a maze of flashing lights, all mingling together in some kind of a dream pattern.

Peter sat in the passenger's seat, completely oblivious to what was going on around him. He played with the three pistols instead, loading and reloading the weapons, humming inanely to himself.

"Now remember," Don was saying, trying to sound cold and authoritative, "we shoot without asking questions. Just blow those fucking niggers to hell. You got that?"

Peter nodded with an idiot's grin plastered across his face. "Yeah, far out . . . ."

Don concentrated hard on the highway and finally managed to drive the car to the rear of the Palmwood Gardens apartments. He stopped next to the curb and shut off the engine.

"This is it," he said.

"Far out . . . ." Peter replied, handing Don a pistol. "They're all ready to go. Just pull the fucking trigger."

The two young white men staggered from the car, and weaved their way toward the rear entrance to the parking lot. Both tried to focus beneath the harsh glare of the overhead lights, but the quaaludes had made reality little more than a swirling mass of figures and shapes. They continued on, however.

Churchman checked his watch for the thousandth time. It was nearly eleven o'clock. One more hour and he would have to make his move. The speed which he had taken earlier was now in full effect. His senses were keen, and he was wound tight like a cougar ready to pounce on his prey. With controlled breathing and a heightened sense of anticipation, Churchman stood next to the pick-up truck, ready. He would wait one more hour.

Lenny and Jason climbed down the stairs, each man holding a suitcase. They waited until a couple crossed the path in front of them before exposing themselves to the courtyard. Using the suitcases as shields, they walked quickly past the pool and the Jacuzzi toward the stairway which led to the garage.

Each man held a .38 in his free hand, the safety latch off and the gun ready to fire. They knew that Churchman was waiting in the shadows, somewhere. But they had to take the chance of exposing themselves in order to get to Los Angeles. There, at least, they would have a fighting change.

Lenny was the first to spot Don and Peter weaving toward them from the far end of the garage. He and Jason had already descended the stairs and were on level ground.

"Drop!" Lenny called to Jason.

Both men fell to their knees, holding their suitcases in front of them at eye level.

Both Don and Peter saw the two black men drop to their knees at the base of the stairs. The two youths raised their guns in unison and began firing.

Churchman stepped out from behind the pick-up truck and leveled his .38 at the backs of Jason and Lenny. The confusion of the moment, with the appearance of the white men, had made Churchman hesitate. He could have hit both Jason and Lenny before they reached the bottom of the stairs, but he had not because of the appearance of Don and Peter.

Peter saw the large black man firing in open range next to the pick-up truck. He turned his aim away from Lenny and Jason, took dead aim and fired two rounds.

Churchman felt the bullets riddle his belly. The force of their entry shocked him enough so that he dropped his gun. His body crumpled beneath him, and he felt his legs give out. He cursed softly to himself as he melted to the floor. The cold concrete hit him in the face as he dropped. The gunfire continued to blast at his ears.

"Back up the stairs!" Lenny yelled above the roar of the gunshots. In unison, he and Jason backed up the five stairs and found cover behind a huge concrete pillar.

Don and Peter, meanwhile, ducked behind some cars, and continued firing in the general direction of the two black men.

Lenny looked out at the row of cars and could only sight his target by using the source of their gunfire. They were moving from his right to left, toward the front entrance of the garage.

"I think they got Churchman," Lenny whispered during a lull in the shooting.

"Bastards!" Jason replied. He was angry at the fact

that the white boys had killed a brother, even if that brother had been sent to kill them. It was one thing for a black to kill another black, but an entirely different matter when it was a white man who pulled the trigger.

"We got to get those motherfuckers," Lenny breathed.

Jason nodded. "They're heading toward the front. When they pass our wheels, I'll make a break. We can run 'em down and keep on flying right on out of here!"

Churchman used the temporary silence to regain his presence of mind. He knew that he was hit bad, somewhere in the stomach region, and that he was bleeding profusely. His hand was pressed against the wound, trying to keep the blood from flowing rampantly out of his body. His other wound was very close to the first. But he had seen enough men shot to know that if he could halt the bleeding, and get to his car and a doctor, he might live. Beyond that, he could not think. All he knew at the moment was that his survival was at stake, and that he hadn't much time.

Churchman began crawling between the cars toward the front entrance of the garage. He held the keys to his rented Cadillac in his hand where once he had held his gun. Every inch was a struggle, and lashed his body with pain. But he was only a hundred feet or so away from the entrance, and his car was only thirty feet beyond that across the street. He knew he had a good shot at making it.

Don and Peter were almost paralleling Churchman's movements toward the front entrance. They were a row of cars away from him and did not see his hulky body inching its way along the concrete.

Both white men were dazed. The combination of drugs, alcohol and the fear mechanism which the shooting had caused had sent both into a state of shock. They moved like somnambulists behind their cars, whispering softly and desperately to each other without really saying anything.

"Kill the fuckers," Peter mumbled. "Kill 'em. Get us out of here!"

"They can't get us, Peter," Don mumbled. "We're too good. They can't reach us . . . ."

They staggered against each other, and the weight of Don's body pushed Peter out into the open for a brief moment.

Lenny saw the blond head stagger next to a parked Ford. He raised his gun and fired. A terrible scream echoed throughout the parking lot.

"I'm hit!" Peter screamed. Don dropped next to his friend and examined him quickly. Blood was gushing from Peter's upper thigh.

"Oh God!" Don cried, helping Peter to his feet. "We've got to get out of here!" Holding his friend upright, Don staggered toward the street.

Jason used the moment to bolt across the open area to the Chevrolet. He jumped inside, cranked over the engine and pulled the car out of the slot. With screeching tires he drove the long way around the lot to where Lenny waited.

Churchman had reached the middle of the street and had but ten feet to go. The white Cadillac loomed above him like some kind of magical chariot. Churchman groaned as he moved closer, extending the hand in which he carried the keys toward the door.

Suddenly, a foot came down hard on his hand and the keys fell to the asphalt. Churchman looked up into the terrified face of a white boy.

Don leaned down, still holding onto Peter who was sobbing hysterically now, and picked up the keys. He dragged his friend to the Cadillac, and with trembling fingers unlocked the door and opened it.

"Get in!" he screamed as he lay Peter across the front seat. Peter cried out loud now as Don forced his legs into the car and jumped behind them into the driver's seat.

Churchman began crawling backward toward the parking lot. He could not accept the fact that there was nothing more he could do. Movement was his only salvation. He had to keep moving, even though he now had no direction at all. He gritted his teeth and fought off the pain as he reached the sidewalk.

Don fumbled with the ignition for a moment, screaming at Peter all the time. Finally, he managed to insert the key. Before turning it over, he grinned. "We're home!" he shouted.

The explosion ripped the Cadillac into a thousand pieces. Churchman saw pieces of human bodies flying in all directions, flaming like fireballs into the night sky. The concussion hit him an instant later, lifted him off the ground and threw him against a concrete pillar.

The night became filled with the screams and shouts of the men and women from the apartment complex. The Cadillac, what little remained of it, sat torched at the curb, its metal groaning like some wounded beast beneath the heat of the fire.

Jason was just starting to pull away when the car went. He looked to Lenny then back at the huge explosion. "Jesus fuck!" he exclaimed.

"Get the shit outa here!" Lenny screamed.

The people began moving into the garage, running toward the cars with wild gleams in their eyes and the hungry look of tragedy etched across their faces.

Jason screeched through the lot toward the entrance and slammed on his brakes when he saw the hulking figure of Churchman sprawled against a pillar.

"Pick him up!" Lenny screamed.

"You crazy?" Jason yelled.

Lenny did not answer, but flung open the car door and leaped out. He dragged the unconscious hit man to the rear of the car, opened the back door and lifted the huge bulk into the rear seat.

"Okay, let's go," Lenny shouted, but with a calmness to his voice that startled Jason.

The mob had gathered around the burning Cadillac. Jason shut down the lights as he turned onto the street and wailed through the crowd. At least they would have trouble getting a license number, if anyone was astute enough to try.

As they screamed down the long block, Lenny turned back to look at the fiery scene. "So long, Palmwood Gardens," he said softly.

They found a small hospital some five miles away from the complex. It was a modern facility, set back amongst a row of eucalyptus trees. Lenny walked into the front entrance with his gun held firmly in his hand.

"We got a sick man needs help. Now!"

The startled nurse, a woman in her late fifties, stuttered nervously as she called out over the intercom for a doctor.

In a few seconds an elderly white man appeared. He looked calmly at Lenny, then at the gun. "Where is he?" the doctor asked in a quiet, unaffected voice.

"No heroes," Lenny warned.

The doctor shook his head. "I'm no fool," he said simply.

Lenny nodded. "Good. He's out front in the car."

The doctor got two interns to bring a stretcher and had Churchman wheeled into the emergency operating room.

Lenny and Jason stood over the doctor, watching as

he removed the two bullets from Churchman's midsection. The doctor had analyzed the wounds as flesh wounds, saying that they had not hit a vital organ. "He's a very lucky man," he said.

Lenny rocked nervously back and forth on his feet as the interns stitched up the wound.

The doctor shrugged and lit a cigarette. He offered one to Lenny and he took it. "What's your scene, doctor?" Lenny asked after taking a light from the doctor.

The doctor smiled a quirky little smile and puffed on his cigarette. "No scene."

"Yeah, but this whole thing don't seem to affect you at all."

The doctor shrugged again. "It's life, nothing strange about it." Had he had more time, the doctor would have liked to explain to the slender black man why he felt the way he did. Explain what two Asian wars and an uncountable number of massacres had done to his sense of right and wrong. But he did not have the time. And besides, it was nobody's business but his own.

With Churchman lying unconscious in the back seat of the Chevrolet, Jason drove the freeway toward Los Angeles. It wasn't until they could see the skyline of the downtown area that he spoke.

"Why?" he asked simply.

Lenny lit a cigarette for Jason, then one for himself. "We need him," he replied simply.

"Man," Jason exclaimed. "That man's paid to kill the both of us. We don't need that kind of shit!"

"Listen, my man," Lenny began. 'Churchman was set up by Hodding. That explosion was no accident. It was meant for our man back there. Hodding got that kind of rep, but Churchman was too low in the streets to know it."

"We risked our lives, man," Jason complained, "saving that dude's. We sat around that hospital for an hour, man. I don't dig it at all!"

"The man got himself a second change. And besides, he got himself one fine rep. He's strong, loyal, and wants to be on the inside. We got him as ours, now."

Jason shook his head and angrily snuffed out his cigarette in the ashtray.

"Man smart enough to know he's been double-crossed. He'll be loyal as shit to us, Jason. And we need that kind of strength right now. He'll be with us all the way from now on."

"If we ever get rid of this short and hole up in time. Bet every fucking pig in Los Angeles out there looking for us!"

"Maybe," Lenny agreed. "Then maybe they can't figure out what went down back there. I mean, a resort apartment house like that, a Caddy blowing up in their faces. Got to confuse them white folks something terrible."

"Hope you're right, my man. But I still don't think we tripped right by bringing him along."

Lenny stared out the window for a long time. He sighed before he spoke. "You think Churchman out here alone to pull off this hit? Man, you losing some of that street intelligence fast. Man had to have some kind of connection going for him, someone to arrange all that shit. He couldn't of traced our car down as fast as he did without some help. Out there," Lenny continued, gesturing to the skyline of Los Angeles, "we got ourselves one fucked up enemy who wants us dead 'cause Carter Hodding wants us dead. We got to find that dude and get his brains scattered 'fore he does the same to us!"

"Churchman'll help us?" Jason asked.

Lenny nodded. "I know the man. You don't play a dude for a sucker and expect him to protect his sources afterwards. Our man back there only dude in California know anything about Hodding and his people out here. He'll take us right to 'em. And then, my man, we'll get in our licks like we deserve."

Jason drove in silence into the downtown area of Los Angeles. The streets were virtually deserted. Beneath the modern skyscrapers winos and bums sat on the sidewalks, silently watching the Chevrolet move past with vacant, dead eyes.

"Where'll we go?" Jason asked as he turned on Hill Street toward the east.

"Just keep driving, my man. We got to get to the darkest, lowest part of this city. At least till we get rid of this short."

They drove another ten miles to the south, down Avalon Boulevard and into the ghetto area commonly known as Watts. A small motel on a side street seemed perfect. They pulled in, slipped the old toothless black man who ran the place a fifty, and no questions were asked.

And then, like two parents, they carried an unconscious Churchman into the small, dingy room and put him into the one bed.

CHAPTER FOURTEEN

THE LITTLE ROOM at the small motel was quite a change from the Palmwood Gardens apartments. But at least it was safe, and no one knew where they were.

For two whole days, Lenny and Jason sat inside the room, tending to a quickly recovering Churchman, drinking and playing cards. Even the television worked badly, so there wasn't much time watching the rash of weekend football games.

It was late Sunday night when Lenny decided to make his first move. "I'm going to score some coke," he said flatly as Jason dealt another hand of gin.

"You mean, now?" Jason asked.

Lenny nodded. "I got to get our contact set up fast down here. There going to be a big hole left when Hodding's people are out of it."

Jason smiled. "Man, you got yourself some kind of plans."

"Yeah," Lenny agreed. "Learned myself a lot out

182

here. Streets ain't as ugly as New York, but the people just as mean. Figure we watch ourselves and a couple of young bucks like you and me make a killing.''

"Right on," Jason enthused, taking his partner's hand.

They had unloaded the Chevrolet the moment they had settled into the motel, cleaning the car of fingerprints and dumping it in an abandoned parking lot. Los Angeles was covered with used car lots, and it was easy enough to pick up a used car for cash. Lenny had bought a three year old Ford, complete with a stereo tape deck and air conditioning. Now, as he pulled out of the motel parking lot, he inserted a tape of Miles Davis which he had picked up and rolled up the windows to ward off the Los Angeles heat.

He drove across town to West Hollywood and to the sight of his first cocaine score. The street was virtually filled with young men all wearing Levis and tank top shirts. "The Western fag," Lenny chuckled to himself as the young men stared into the car as he drove past. He pulled up in front of a small bar, locked the car and went inside.

The room was dark, and a Bette Midler album was playing on the juke box. A thin blond man wearing a skin tight tee shirt swished up to the bar.

"What'll you have?" he asked in a lispy voice.

Lenny had to keep himself from laughing. The guy was almost too much of a stereotype to be real. "A beer," Lenny replied.

The bartender nodded, smiled, and poured out a draft. Lenny drank slowly, searching the faces of the men around the bar, looking for the dude he and Jason had bought the coke from the first time around. Suddenly a hand rested lightly on his shoulder. Lenny swung around and looked into the light blue eyes of the man he was looking for.

"Came back alone?" the youth said.

Lenny smiled. "Hey little brother, hoped I'd find you hanging out here."

"My name's Jim," he said. "And I told you you could always find me here." Jim took the stool next to Lenny and casually let his hand fall on Lenny's knee. With a firm grip, Lenny removed his hand.

"Just business, my man," Lenny said in a friendly voice.

Jim smiled. "A shame. A damned shame. Some of the best always go to waste."

"Yeah, well, this dude's not wasting his stuff on nothin' that don't have a pussy."

This made Jim laugh. "Okay, what do you need?"

"Coke," Lenny replied simply.

"How much?"

"How big can you go?"

Jim turned away and thought for a moment. "Unlimited?" he said. His voice was now stern, and the softness had gone out of it. He was all business.

"Unlimited," Lenny repeated.

"Okay. I can do five ounces right now. More later. Five at an even eighty-five hundred. That's including my cut."

Lenny nodded. "Sounds fair enough. How soon?"

"I told you," Jim replied. "Immediately."

Lenny took Jim's hand and led him to the restroom. The other men in the bar watched with envious smiles on their faces. Jim winked at them as he strode by.

Inside the head, Lenny locked the door. He fished into his wallet and pulled out eighty-five hundred dollars in cash. "I'll want some cut with this shit," he said as he handed the money to Jim.

Jim nodded. "I'll see what I can do." He took the

money and stuffed it into the pocket of his Levis.

Lenny started to leave, but Jim grabbed his wrist. "A little more time, to make it look like the real thing."

Lenny smiled and lit a cigarette.

Two hours later, and three propositions later, Lenny was still sitting at the bar, nursing his sixth beer. He began to wonder if he hadn't made a terrible mistake. Jim was, after all, a total stranger, a man whom Lenny had met only once before. But then again, there was the fact that Lenny knew what the homosexual's hangout was, and who his friends were inside the bar. It struck Lenny that it was also strange that Jim had trusted him. Possibly this was the only way to do business on the West Coast. Whatever the situation, Lenny had to take the chance.

Jim entered the bar a few minutes later, smiling broadly. He walked up to Lenny and put his arm around his shoulder. "All set," he said in a sing-song voice.

Lenny nodded, paid his bar tab and stood up. He followed Jim to the parking lot across the street from the bar. Jim drove an old Volkswagen, and Lenny climbed into the front seat with him.

"You're a very lucky dude," Jim said as he opened a black briefcase. "I'm well known around here, my contacts are huge. Anyone else and you would have had hell's time getting this shit."

"I appreciate it," Lenny said.

Jim pulled out five small baggies filled with the white powder. "Everything's here," he said. "The cut's procaine. One ounce, on the house. I told my main man that it appeared as if we'd be doing quite a business together. He offered the cut as a symbol of his desire to continue the relationship.

Lenny nodded. "Tell him that I plan to become one

of the biggest in the south central district. And if I move into any of his areas, please let me know. Tell him that the area is controlled out of New York, but that very quickly that control will be mine."

Jim listened intently. "I will tell him," he said. "And I am sure he'll respect your considerations."

Lenny shook the man's hand and started out of the car. He stopped just before opening the door. "One thing, man," Lenny began.

"Yeah, Lenny?"

"I mean, you doin' alright. Obviously you got some heavy duty shit put together down here. Why hang around street corners?"

Jim smiled weakly. "When you're like I am, man, sometimes you can't help yourself. Let's just say I try to combine as much pleasure with my business as possible."

"I can dig it," Lenny nodded. "Be rappin' at you soon."

Lenny carried the briefcase casually across the street and got into his Ford. He whistled as he drove away. It was the easiest score he had ever made in his life.

When he entered the motel room, Churchman was sitting up in bed and being spoon fed chicken soup by Jason. Lenny chuckled at the sight. "Never thought I'd see one of the meanest niggers in Harlem sittin' up in bed like some kind of baby!"

Jason giggled. Churchman glared at Lenny, then pushed the soup away.

"What the fuck's going on here?" he asked in a low, gruff voice.

Lenny put the briefcase on the kitchen table and opened it. He took one of the bags and threw it at Churchman. Churchman held the bag in his hands, turning it over and over, examining it.

"Eighty percent pure coke," Lenny said lightly. "One full ounce, Churchman. And with a proper cut, five thousand big ones on the street."

Churchman looked to Jason, then to Lenny. "What you gonna do, man, blow my head off with this stuff 'fore you put me away?"

"Shit!" Lenny exclaimed. "Man don't know his friends when he see them! Goddamn, man, me and Jason risked our black asses to get you in one piece out of that fucking set-up! Shit!"

Churchman smiled for the first time. His teeth were crooked, but his smile was open and friendly. "I was really put up back there, wasn't I?" he said.

"I'd say so, my man," Lenny agreed. "Carter Hodding got a rep on his ass for things like that. Surprised you weren't hip to it."

"Surprised you dudes didn't just blow me away. Had a contract on you both."

Lenny threw out his hands and shrugged. "Business, Churchman, strictly business. I'd say right now, you ain't got no contract no more. Wouldn't you agree?"

"Yeah, it kinda looks that way alright."

"Ain't no two ways about it, my man. And that coke you got there in your hands? That's just a way of saying welcome to the organization.

"Shit, you're putting me on?"

"No way," Lenny laughed. "And don't get no paranoid notions about it neither. If I was going to give you a kiss of death, I wouldn't spend no two grand to do it. No man, you know what Jason and my reps are like."

Churchman nodded slowly. "I know people on the street always say you both good for your word."

"Well," Lenny said, "you can count on it. We come out here to get a few things straight, and get away from Hodding's guns. We ain't quite out of the way yet, but as soon as we do we going to start making some noise in L.A."

Jason watched his partner closely, lighting a cigarette and holding back on his comments. He was waiting to see in what direction Lenny was going to take Churchman.

"Now," Lenny began, "we got ourselves some good plans. A little coke, some dope in the form of pills, shit like that. I got me a fine bunch of contacts down in Orange County to make us a fortune. Problem is, I got my feelings about Carter Hodding out here. Feel like he's got a thing going, you dig where I'm coming from?"

Churchman nodded.

"I mean, the whole set-up with you. Had to have some powerful dudes ready to roll out here to pull that off, didn't he?

Churchman glanced around the room. "You want the cat," he began in a low voice, "I'll give him to you. And I don't need to get paid with no cocaine neither. I owe it to myself, and to you dudes for pulling me out."

Jason nodded to Lenny. For the first time, Jason was beginning to trust Churchman.

"Man," Lenny replied, "ain't no need to throw away a little fun, my man. The good times are gonna roll, and you gonna roll right with them. You dig where I'm coming from?"

Churchman grinned. "I'm with you all the way, my man. If that's the way you want it."

Lenny extended his hand and clasped Churchman's. Jason moved over to the bed and put his hand over the other two.

"The name," Churchman said evenly, "is Clinton Jones."

For two young dudes on the streets looking to score a whole lot of cocaine, finding Clinton Jones was not a difficult matter. Lenny and Jason began at the Parisian Room, a small, well known nightclub near La Brea in downtown L.A. Dressed in their finest, they entered the jazz spot on a hot Tuesday night. Gloria Lynn was due to hold down on center stage, and the place was jammed.

In New York, it was the bartenders who served as connections to the men who were in need. It took some casual conversation, a couple of key words, and normally, the bartender would respond with what the hungry soul needed. Lenny left his table and sauntered to the wide, curving bar to see if the same action was possible in Los Angeles.

"What's happenin'?" the man behind the bar asked. He was a young black, wearing an expensive silk shirt and, Lenny noticed, a solid gold bracelet. Like most men who tended drinks, Lenny figured this one had a lot going on the side.

Lenny smiled and took a seat. The stools next to him were empty, and the music in the background softly played by a trio. It was still too early for Gloria Lynn. "Have a beer," Lenny said quietly.

The bartender nodded, poured a draft and slid it across the bar.

"Nice place here," Lenny commented as he sipped from the beer.

"One of the best," the bartender commented. The man's sixth sense was already working, he could feel Lenny's interest.

"Kind of place where a man might be able to get most anything," Lenny continued.

The bartender laughed. "All depends on what that man looking for. Some things real easy to get, others not so easy."

The bartender looked straight at Lenny, sizing him up. His mind recorded certain thoughts—young, good-looking, but definitely off the streets. He detected a New York clip to Lenny's voice, and surmised that he was recently moved to the West Coast.

"You new around here?" the bartender asked.

Lenny nodded. "Yeah. Just came in from the East. Looking for some party action with my friend over there." Lenny gestured to the table where Jason sat sipping a whiskey.

"Well," the bartender smiled, "you dudes got the money, it possible to have one hell of a time in L.A. No doubt . . . ."

Lenny leaned across the bar and in close. "We got money, my man, plenty of money. And good time's all we after."

"Okay," the bartender said. "What you need?"

"Women and dope," Lenny grinned. "Plenty of dope and just two women."

"Lots of kind of dope," the bartender replied.

"Not like the pure white gold coming off them mountains of South America," Lenny responded. "You dig where I'm coming from?"

The bartender smiled again. "The pause that refreshes. No problem. How much?"

"Five grams, my man," Lenny chirped.

The bartender raised his eyebrows. Normally, the contacts wanted, at most, two grams. The high rollers had better contacts and did not work through him. "You really new in town, ain't you?" he said after a long silence.

"Told you, my man, we just got in."

"Go back to your table, enjoy the show, and I'll let you know what I find out."

Lenny slid a fifty dollar bill across the bar. "There's more where that coming from, my man. Much more. Me and my partner do appreciate your efforts."

The bartender picked up the bill and slid it quickly into his pocket. "You do know how to do business, my man," he grinned. "And by the way, name's Leroy."

Lenny shook the man's hand. "Call me Julius," he said.

Jason lit a cigarette as his partner sat down. "What's going down?" he asked quickly.

"Man knows his business. He's checking it out right now. Way I figure it, Carter Hodding's man, Clinton Jones, should be the main man in this area of town. We get to one of his pushers, we get to him."

"How you know all that, my man?" Jason asked.

Lenny grinned. "Hodding's lady told me. Said as how Hodding had this dream of building an empire out here based entirely on coke. It would stand to figure that Clinton Jones be his main man. I mean, he trusted Jones with wiping out Churchman, didn't he?"

Jason turned very serious, staring down at the whiskey in his glass. "Man, we hit Jones and Hodding really going to come after our asses, ain't he?"

"Organization too small out here yet. You got to remember, that was only six months ago Hodding set it up. Way I figure it, we be able to deal with Hodding once we eliminate his top fool."

"Man," Jason smiled, "from Palmwood Gardens to this. We sure doing some travelin', my man."

Lenny leaned back and lit a cigarette. "You'd better believe. Now relax and enjoy the sounds. I think we probably got ourselves a little wait."

Just prior to the main act coming on stage, one of the busboys leaned over Lenny's shoulder and whispered into his ear. Lenny nodded, slipped him a five dollar bill and walked to the bar.

The bartender slid a piece of paper across the bar to Lenny. On it was an address, an apartment on Hoover Street in downtown Los Angeles.

"Man's name is Cletus," the bartender said. "He's waitin' for you right now."

Lenny smiled and slid another fifty across the bar. "I appreciate this quick service, my man," he said.

"You want some foxes, my man, just come on back. I'll keep some of the ladies who show up here waitin'."

"You do that. We goin' to party all night long!"

Lenny and Jason drove across town and into a heavily industrialized area. The apartment on Hoover street was a run-down affair, situated between two large warehouses. Both Lenny and Jason checked their .38s before leaving the car and entering the building.

They walked the two flights to the third floor. The hallways were dim and the ceiling cracked.

"Can't believe a man deals in expensive shit like this and lives in a fucking hole!"

Lenny knocked on apartment three and waited. The door opened a crack, and a man's deep voice asked who it was.

"Cletus? This here's Leroy and my running partner."

Cletus pulled the latch off the door and opened it. He was a short man, and very skinny. His eyes were large and soft. His skin seemed to shine, and Lenny knew immediately what his style was. Heroin.

"Come on in," Cletus said.

Lenny and Jason entered the neat little apartment. A young black girl, also thin and with the same sheen about her, sat on the bed. She smoked a cigarette and smiled at Lenny and Jason.

"My man," Cletus began, "said you dudes interested

in some fine shit."

"Man's right," Lenny said. "We doin' some good partyin' tonight. Need about five . . . ."

Cletus smiled. "Ain't no problem. My man mentioned the figure, and I sent out. Cokeman, he delivers."

Lenny chuckled. "And what's the charge?"

"Five yards, straight up and down."

Lenny fished into his pocket and pulled out a wad of bills. He peeled off five hundred dollar bills and handed them to Cletus. "Fair enough, my man."

The roll of bills had caught Cletus' eye, as it had his woman's. They exchanged glances. "Okay, five big ones," Cletus said. He walked across the small room to his dresser and pulled out five folded pieces of brown paper. He lay them out on top of the dresser and stepped back. "Take a try, my man," he said.

Lenny chose the packet on the far right, opened it carefully and cut away some of the white powder with a razor blade. Cletus had everything ready for use. The straw was a gold plated one, and Lenny used it to snort the coke. He smiled as he sniffed the stuff deeper into his nervous system.

"Not bad, my man," Lenny said. "Not bad at all."

Cletus nodded to Jason. After repeating the ritual, Jason agreed with his partner.

"Glad everything's cool," Cletus said. "I'm always around for whatever you want, you dig?"

Lenny put the packets into his pocket slowly, then pulled out his wad of bills. Cletus' eyes devoured the money. "I need some information, Cletus," Lenny began slowly. " 'Bout a man named Clinton Jones."

Cletus blanched at the name.

"Me and my partner," Lenny continued, "come all the way out here from Chicago. We got something the man might want. We know he's one of the biggest dudes on the West Coast." Lenny continued playing with the money.

"Information like that costs bread," Cletus said.

Lenny almost laughed. He knew a dude like Jones wouldn't be too hard to find if they had the time. But L.A. was a big city, and they had to move fast. Lenny pulled out three hundred dollar bills and lay them on the top of the dresser.

"I don't want his fucking home address, my man. Just where he parties."

Cletus reached out for the money. "The Lion's Den on the Strip, man. You hip to that place?"

"I'll find it, Cletus," Lenny replied.

Lenny nodded to Jason, and the two men walked quickly out of the apartment. Lenny knew that Cletus would be on the phone immediately to Jones. But with his lead at the Lion's Den, it wouldn't be difficult to trace the man down, even if he was aware that they were both looking for him.

The Lion's Den was at the far end of the Strip, sitting on a corner just before Sunset snaked into Beverly Hills. It was a small, intimate club, and most of the clientele was black. A trio played in the center of the room, with tables and a bar encircling it.

Lenny and Jason moved quickly to the bar and leaned across toward the bartender.

"What'll you cats have?" the bartender asked.

"Clinton Jones," Lenny said loudly.

The bartender took a step backward and searched the club frantically.

"I said, we looking for Clinton Jones!"

A huge black man, dressed in a conservative black suit, moved up next to Lenny and leaned against the bar. "I know Clinton Jones," he said softly.

Lenny nodded. "Okay. Tell the man that Lenny and Jason got nine lives, and Churchman don't. And tell him that we might be able to soothe the anger of a Mr. Hodding in New York."

The huge black man nodded. "Is that it?"

Lenny smiled. "Nope. Tell him if he want to be the richest man in L.A., best he set up a meeting. A business meeting."

"That's cool," the black man said, turning to the bartender. "Put their drinks on Mr. Jones' tab." He nodded to Lenny and Jason and moved out of the bar.

Lenny and Jason stood at the bar for two hours, drinking straight whiskeys. Near midnight, the bartender approached Lenny. "You got a phone call," he said simply.

"This is a representative of Clinton Jones," the voice on the other end said quickly. "Mr. Jones would like to meet with you tomorrow night."

"Where?" Lenny asked.

"The Arco Plaza downtown, next to the fountain. He sends his regards, and says he is looking forward to seeing both of you and Jason at eleven-thirty."

Before Lenny could answer, the phone went dead.

"Tomorrow night," Lenny said as he sat down next to Jason. "Now let's split this joint before the man decides to hit us here."

Churchman lay on the bed, watching an old western on the barely workable television. He ate fried chicken and sipped on whiskey. Lenny and Jason barged into the room.

"How you doin', my man?" Lenny asked.

Churchman nodded. "Gettin' itchy sittin' here."

"Ain't no problem, my man." Lenny grinned. "We got some coke, and we got some plans."

"You found him?" Churchman asked, a note of surprise in his voice.

"Man's accessible," Lenny said easily. "Big dudes like that, with shitty operations like he run, they always accessible. Kind of surprised at Carter Hodding, though, letting crap roll on the streets of L.A. like Clinton Jones. Man's a lightweight."

Churchman shook his head. "Got to move carefully. Man got some heavy duty connections out here. What's up with him?"

"We got ourselves a meeting tomorrow night at the Arco Plaza in downtown. You ever seen the place?"

"Nope," Churchman replied.

"Well then," Lenny said. "I suggest we do up a couple lines of this fine shit and take ourselves a quick ride."

They drove through the empty streets of the downtown area and found themselves at the base of the huge black towers. The buildings sat next to each other, with a plaza at the bottom. The fountain burst forth with a spectrum of colors, even at this late hour.

Lenny got out of the car and walked slowly around the fountain, looking up at the huge towers. Churchman and Jason waited inside the car, watching the deserted streets for any sign of a patrol car.

"Man's got something on his mind," Churchman commented.

Jason nodded. "Lenny's always got his head working, man. He's going to be big here."

Churchman smiled. "Glad I didn't carry out my contract, Jason," he said.

"We all got down a little on this one," Jason said philosophically.

"Yeah," Churchman nodded. "Ain't no lie."

Lenny returned to the car, smiling broadly. "You ever use a high-powered rifle with a telescopic sight, my man?" he asked Churchman.

The huge black man leaned out of the car and looked up the forty stories to the top of the towers. "Yeah, I can handle it," he said.

"First thing in the morning, we go buy one," Lenny said as he jumped in behind the wheel. "We hit fast and with no question. It's as simple as that."

"I can dig that, Lenny," Churchman bellowed from the back seat. "I can dig that!"

CHAPTER FIFTEEN

CLINTON JONES stared out the picture window overlooking the Los Angeles basin from his Baldwin Hills home. The night was clear and bright and the lights of Los Angeles twinkled beneath a starry sky. Normally, it would have been a night for partying, for bringing up a few good-looking girls and inviting some friends. But on this beautiful summer night, Clinton Jones was worried. The word had come from the Lion's Den that Lenny and Jason were looking for him. Jones realized that Churchman must have been killed during his attempt on the two young men's lives. What bothered him most was the fact that sooner or later Carter Hodding would find out what had happened in Los Angeles. And when he did, the small empire which he had built with Clinton Jones as its king would collapse. It was a shaky turf upon which the black man walked.

The three large men sat on the sofa and sipped quietly at their drinks, waiting for Jones to speak. They had never seen a man so quiet, so withdrawn as he was now. Each man, a high-ranking officer in the Jones empire, knew something big was happening. But what it was, they weren't sure.

Finally, Clinton Jones turned away from the scenic view and faced his men. He looked at each man individually. Rufus, Lincoln and Emory . . . three of the strongest, most ruthless men in Jones' employ. Each man capable of handling whatever form of violence might arise.

"Okay," Jones began in a subdued voice. "It ain't for a party that I asked you dudes here tonight."

The three men laughed softly.

"We got problems," Jones continued after the laughter died. "Carter Hodding, my main man in New York City, has expressed the desire to eliminate two dudes who put the make on his lady and destroyed his personal life. I'm telling you all this because I don't believe a man should be asked to kill without knowing why."

"We appreciate that," Rufus said, the other two nodding their approval.

"Good," Jones replied. "Now, we got to move on this thing tomorrow night. The cat from New York was blown away trying. It ain't as easy as it seems."

Lincoln lit a cigarette. "What you want, Clinton?" he asked.

"Tomorrow night, I'm having a meeting with these two cats at the Arco towers in downtown L.A. I want to get hip to what they're up to, then simply blow them away. I don't want no fuck ups this time, and I don't want to jive around with these dudes. You dig?"

The three men nodded.

"It's a basic hit, and we all going to be on it. Afterwards, we come back here and party a little," Clinton smiled. "And you know how good my parties are."

"Last time," Emory whistled, "I had me three of the finest things I ever saw!"

"You do me this favor, my man, and you get four!"

The men laughed. Clinton raised his hand to silence them. "Now, I know that ain't the usual kind of shit. It's a personal favor to me. There's no bread in it, there ain't nothing but loyalty involved. But I swear to you cats, you pull this one down, you all going to be well taken care of. Dig?"

Lincoln got to his feet. Slow and lumbering, he was deceiving. Once he was directed, his actions became lithe and athletic. "We all with you, Clinton, you can dig on that!"

Clinton Jones smiled. "Rufus?" he asked.

The heavyset, mean-looking black man smiled and nodded.

"Emory?" Jones asked, looking at the slim black man with the huge Afro. Emory nodded.

"Okay, we all stay here in the pad for the night and tomorrow. There's plenty of football on the tube, so we won't get uptight. Lots of liquor in the cabinet for the evening, but I want everyone sober when we make our move tomorrow night. Dig?"

"Hear that coming ruins the energy," Emory joked.

Clinton smiled. "Better after the job's done, my man. Always . . . ."

Clinton Jones left his three men in the living room and retired to the den. He sat down in the huge leather chair next to the stereo and lit a cigarette. His position at the moment was undefined. Lenny and Jason wanted to talk, about what, he didn't know. But there was a possibility that they were running scared, and if that was the case they could prove to be valuable assets within his small organization. So far, Clinton Jones had been able to secure only losers. The three men sitting in his living room were the exceptions. On his payroll were junkies, hookers and small time con men. Los Angeles was a big city, and a man with brains could score real big in it. Clinton Jones, ever since being sent to the west coast by Carter Hodding, had dreams of becoming that man with brains. Lenny and Jason were obviously shrewd enough to outwit one of Hodding's hit men. Clinton Jones figured that they might make a good addition to his empire. He would talk with them in twenty-four hours. If they were bent on revenge, then he would have his men blow them away. If not, then he would continue talking.

On Sunday mornings the Arco Plaza was virtually empty. The weekday crowds, young men and women who worked in the huge office buildings, had scattered to the suburbs, leaving the fountain and the two glass towers to the less fortunate from the inner depths of Los Angeles' skid row. Now these men sat in worn clothes around the fountain, small brown paper bags tucked neatly between their legs. They all turned and watched their vacant interest as three well-dressed black men strode easily onto the plaza.

"This is it," Lenny said softly. "By the fountain."

Churchman stopped and glanced upward. The two towers loomed into the smoggy sky. Between them were bridges, apparently on the third, fifth and seventh floors. Above that was glass until the rooftops.

"What you think, my man?" Lenny asked.

"Those bridges, Lenny. The roof is too high, I'd never get a shot from way up there."

Jason stepped off the paces to the edge of the fountain, stopped and glanced upward, then returned to the group. "You'd better go as high as you can, Churchman. That water going to be tough to shoot through."

Churchman nodded, then followed his two partners into the main entrance and then into the lobby of the building. The elevators were working, and they rode to the seventh floor. Once there, they walked down a long hallway then came to an open doorway which led out onto the bridge.

"Looks like they built this whole damn thing for our convenience," Lenny laughed.

The three men leaned over the edge and looked down onto the plaza below. They could easily make out the figures of the winos sitting on the other side of the fountain. Churchman cupped his hand to his eye and panned the scene, as though a film director planning a shot. "No problem from up here," he said evenly.

"Too easy," Lenny said, seriously now. "If Jones don't put a plant up here, too, he's dumber than I figured."

"We can't stop him," Jason said. "We just got to hope he don't want to use this particular bridge. If we try and stop him, we'll blow everything."

"No doubt, my man," Lenny mused. "So, once again, we got to be prepared for the strike. I mean, we got to move fast and quickly. Dig? Don't give them motherfuckers a chance!"

Churchman listened to Lenny as he smoked a cigarette.

"Now," Lenny continued, gesturing down to the plaza below. "When me and Jason confront the motherfucker, you shoot. Don't hesitate for one minute. That motherfucker probably got the same notions we got about this whole thing."

Churchman nodded. "I'll be here and I'll be ready.

But what about the security guards? They got to be security guards up here."

"You do what you have to do, my man," Lenny offered. "Ain't no way we can fix that shit before we go tonight. We just got to hope them dudes too lame to see us."

"Hope you're right, my man," Churchman said. "I don't want to have to kill but one man tonight. Wasting some innocent dude ain't my style."

"Mine neither, Churchman," Lenny agreed. "So let's just hope we don't have to get involved with any of that shit, okay?"

"You got it," Churchman grinned.

They drove back through Los Angeles and stopped at a sporting goods store which Lenny had scouted earlier. The manager, a white man in his late fifties, smiled too broadly when Lenny entered the store.

"Have you decided yet?" the manager beamed.

Lenny pulled out his money and threw it on the counter. "I'd like the rifle, with the telescopic sight, my man."

The manager lay the huge rifle on the glass counter. Lenny picked up the gun, checked the sight and the bolt action, then pressed it to Churchman. Churchman handled the gun expertly, and when he finished he nodded to Lenny.

"We'll take it," Lenny said finally.

The manager nodded and put a stack of papers on the counter. "You'll have to fill these out," he said.

Lenny dropped two hundred dollars onto the papers and smiled. "Me and my partners ain't got time, my man. We got to hunt for some deer and filling out all those papers would delay us something awful."

The manager shook his head slowly. "It's the law," he said.

Lenny sighed, and put another hundred dollars onto the countertop.

The manager smiled, scooped up the money and pulled the papers off the counter. "Well, I guess that about takes care of everything," he said simply.

"Guess so," Lenny smiled. He picked up the box of shells and turned to leave the store. Churchman followed him, carrying the rifle over his shoulder. Jason waited for them in the car out front. His .38 lay on the front seat next to him, within easy reach.

"Everything alright?" Jason asked as Lenny and Churchman climbed into the car.

"Everybody got their price," Lenny said. "An' we got the bread to pay it. Going to be easy pickings after tonight."

The three men drove to a steak house on Pico Boulevard and spent a large part of the afternoon eating and watching football games on the oversized television screen. They drank only iced coffees, and spoke in low, subdued tones.

"I don't know about you dudes," Lenny said after the last game was over, "but there's a space movie I saw down the street I'd sure like to see 'bout now."

Churchman smiled and shook his head. "Probably better than sitting around."

"Got to believe it," Lenny said.

They walked the block and a half to the theater and went inside. The cavernous old room was filled with kids, most of them thoroughly entranced with the comings and goings of the spaceships and saucers. Lenny bought popcorn and Cokes and the three men sat in the dark munching away like typically avid moviegoers.

By the time the film was over it was getting dark. The heat of the day had not abated, and a soft wind from the desert drove the temperature even higher.

They drove back to the motel, showered and changed clothing.

"Best we pack our belongings, gentlemen," Lenny said. "We ain't coming back here."

"What you mean, Lenny? Where we going to go?" Jason seemed worried for the moment.

Lenny grinned. "You'll find out about twelve tonight, after the fireworks. Got a little surprise planned for my main men."

Churchman sat on the edge of the bed, resting the rifle on his thighs. "You sure about me, Lenny?" he asked. "I mean, maybe it's best I kind of get my ass out of.L.A. for awhile."

"And go where? New York? Man, ain't no way you leaving our side, 'less of course you want to take some foxy broad to Vegas or something. There may or may not be heat after tonight. If there is, I want you with me. You dig?"

The large, homely black man had a way of putting himself down, of being just a little too humble. The attitude angered Lenny, he didn't have time for that kind of thing. He figured that Churchman, because of his looks, had always felt like an outsider. Thus, the attitude. He just hoped that after tonight the hit man would forget about his personal feelings and just do his job. Lenny could not deal with insecurity in a man, especially a trigger man.

By ten o'clock they were packed, dressed and ready to move. Lenny paid the bill at the office and the three men moved out. They reached the Arco Plaza ten minutes later. The skies of Los Angeles had cleared as a result of the desert winds, and the towers loomed huge and beautiful against the starry sky. Lenny drove around the plaza twice, then stopped near the entrance which they had used the day before.

Lenny turned to Churchman who sat in the back seat, his rifle resting in his lap, covered with a simple bedsheet they had stolen from the motel. "You'll have yourself about fifty minutes up there," Lenny began. "Me and Jason will be back about five minutes after ten . . . want the man to think we playing for power and really want to talk."

Churchman nodded and lit a cigarette. Lenny noticed that his hands were steady, his eyes very clear and sharp. "Now, the moment you hit Jones," Lenny continued, "me and Jason will get his bodyguards. But there is a real possibility they will back right on off. I know these kinds of dudes, and Jones been running a shabby organization. They probably ready to come with us, and if that's the case we could use them. So just keep awake up there, watch what's going on down here.

"I'll leave the gun up there," Churchman began, picking up where Lenny had left off, "use the stairs and come directly out into the plaza."

"Me and Jason'll be waiting. And unless there's a cop sitting in that fucking fountain, we shouldn't have no troubles from the police."

"Okay," Churchman said. "I guess that's it, then."

" 'Bout it, my man," Lenny countered. "We'll see you in about an hour."

Churchman nodded to Lenny, then to Jason. Quickly, and with more agility than Lenny had seen in the man before, he bounded from the car and walked casually, but very quickly across the plaza and into the main entrance of the building. Lenny waited until he disappeared into the stairwell before pulling out.

They drove slowly through the deserted streets of downtown Los Angeles, smoking cigarettes and talking rapidly.

Jason seemed incredibly nervous, and Lenny knew he

would have to keep the man talking. "It seem like we made all the right moves since we got out here," Lenny said enthusiastically. "Everything we touch turning to gold. Now, I know we can't count on that kind of luck all the time, but a little bit sure don't hurt us none."

Jason nodded and stared vacantly out the window of the car at the run down, empty buildings. "This city just like all the others. Falling apart at the seams."

Lenny laughed. "Don't let that shit fool you, my man. Lot of people putting money in here. And we going to help ourselves to a little bit of it."

Jason smiled, pulled his .38 from his pocket and examined the gun one more time. Satisfied, he stuffed it back into his pocket.

They drove for another half hour, this time in silence. Jason lit a cigarette and inhaled deeply. "Lenny?" he began in a soft voice.

"What it is, my man?"

"Who's to say Churchman won't hit us?"

Lenny chuckled. "You don't know human nature none too well, my man. Churchman got to go with the man who give him the order. Maybe it's because he's ugly or something, but his whole life he been used to taking orders from someone. And besides, the man does have his pride. He was turned around by Carter Hodding pretty bad. He'll hit Jones, Jason, don't you worry none about that."

"It just seems like we takin' one awful chance, Lenny."

Lenny sighed. "Shit, we got to, Jason. We playing for some awfully high stakes here. It's the name of the game, my man."

Jason turned away from his friend and once again regarded the Los Angeles streets. Lenny's overconfident manner had oftentimes bothered him tremendously. But the facts were proving Lenny right. They were in much better shape since their arrival to the West Coast, and now there was a possibility of really setting themselves up in something big. Although Jason was not as secure about the outcome as his partner, he knew that his best odds were to ride with Lenny.

Lenny had always been able to sense the lack of confidence in his friend, and he had always managed to restore it. The key to Jason, Lenny knew, was the past. In a friendly tone, he began recounting the stories of their years together, from the beginning some twenty years ago in the streets of Harlem. There had been trouble then, plenty of it, and the two running partners had always managed to pull themselves out without much damage being inflicted on them. That history of moving in and out of trouble had given Lenny confidence, and now he used that same history to reinstill confidence in his friend.

Jason listened to the stories and nodded, then began smiling. "You playing with me, Lenny," he chided easily. "You think I'm worried something awful."

Lenny shrugged. "Man would be crazy not to be worried a little. We about ready to hit a big man in L.A. It ain't your everyday situation."

"You a little uptight, then?" Jason asked.

Lenny grinned at his partner. " 'Course I am. I ain't crazy."

Jason laughed and shook his head. "Time moving on, my man. Best we get over there and get our business taken care of."

"You got it, my man," Lenny exclaimed. "You got it!"

Clinton Jones had sent a man to the Palmwood Gardens apartment complex in an attempt to find out what had taken place the night Lenny and Jason were to be hit. The man had spoken with some of the neighbors, and mainly with an old black security guard named Thadius. The report had satisfied Jones. According to the people who lived in the complex, a white Cadillac had exploded, then caught fire, maiming the driver. No one had seen the man who was killed in the fiery holocaust. The police had come and done an investigation, but no one had bothered to check out their reports. Clinton Jones had not secured a contact within the law enforcement agencies of Southern California, and thus had no access to closed police files. So, the version of the story which he received from Orange County was that Churchman was now nothing more than a pile of ashes. Had Clinton Jones been more thorough in his operation, and secured that contact, he would have heard a completely different version. Through the use of teeth impressions, the police had been able to identify the scarred, maimed bodies of the two young white men who had been burned inside the car that night. Both from good families, the police were baffled as to the motive of the crime. They had tried tracing the rented Cadillac, but had come up empty. Clinton Jones, on that count at least, had been thorough.

The report from Orange County and the Palmwood Gardens apartment complex had gratified Clinton Jones. His mind jumped quickly to a conclusion which he had arrived at already. That Lenny and Jason were running scared, feeling like hunted rabbits with the dogs hot on their trail. Clinton Jones felt certain that they wanted to deal, not for profit or gain, but essentially for their lives.

Rufus, Lincoln and Emory stood around the living room of Clinton Jones' Baldwin Hills home, waiting calmly for the word to move. Each man wore a shoulder holster with a .357 magnum securely packaged inside.

They were ready for whatever might come down at the meeting.

But Clinton Jones did not expect the worst. He was flagrantly excited about the meeting. He had a plan which had been forming in his mind ever since the word had come down that Lenny and Jason wanted to talk. It was a plan that he felt was at once devious and brilliant. Clinton Jones, because of the level of his aides and operatives, had an unrealistically high opinion of himself. His plan was very simple. He would offer Lenny and Jason the chance to redeem themselves. Basically, he would allow them to score a huge supply of cocaine, bringing them into his operation in a large way. Then, he would simply kill them both. Carter Hodding would be none the wiser, thinking all the time that Clinton Jones had executed his wishes with efficiency, even though Churchman had been lost to the struggle. And Clinton Jones would be the wealthier through his cocaine score. Clinton Jones was very happy with himself and with his plan as he entered the living room of his home and greeted his three bodyguards.

"One thing before we split," Jones began. "I don't want no trigger happy fucking around. Those boys are coming to beg for their lives, and if I play my guess right, we'll all be able to make a little change off their desire to survive. Dig?"

The three men nodded.

Rufus took a step forward, his face was taut and serious. "I hate to talk like this, Clinton, but it sure seems we should have checked this scene out before going over there."

Clinton put his hand on Rufus' shoulder in a patronizing manner. "I checked out everything, Rufus," he began in a confident voice. "Those two niggers out there all alone, scared shitless. They got New York after their asses, and they got me out here. There's nowhere for them to run. They're powerless. They been in L.A. a week, maybe less. No time to get any kind of action going. I checked with all the cats on the streets, and there's no waves coming down about hiring guns or anything like that. Those boys out there to beg for their lives, my man."

Rufus looked the man squarely in the eye. He had been working for Clinton Jones for just under a year now. His confidence in the man was not the highest. He knew a little of Carter Hodding's operations, and suspected correctly that Jones was a flagship in Los Angeles, a testing explorer sent into the territory to determine where the strengths and weaknesses were. That Clinton Jones himself did not realize this worried Rufus. The man's ego was huge, and Rufus knew that such a state of affairs could easily blind a man.

"Everybody ready?" Clinton Jones asked as he checked his watch. "We got but a half hour to get down there." Clinton Jones turned and walked from the house to the black Lincoln parked in the driveway. He climbed into the passenger seat, Rufus jumped in behind the steering wheel and Emory and Lincoln took the back seat.

Rufus backed the car out of the driveway and headed down the hill toward the Santa Monica freeway and the city center.

Churchman leaned against the concrete wall and lit another cigarette. The rifle rested against the wall next to him. Some seventy feet below the large fountain sprayed water above the bluish green lights. The plaza itself was illuminated brightly by lights, and the wind blew softly through the opening where the bridge linked the two towers.

The large man checked his watch and sighed. It was now five minutes to eleven. So far, Churchman had seen nothing of a security guard, or any life whatsoever in the building.

The fifty minutes he had spent on the bridge had given him time to think. His mind was racing. The events of the last couple weeks had changed his entire life. From the streets of Harlem to the penthouse suite of Carter Hodding to the dreamlike stage of the Palmwood Gardens complex to this. He had blown his assignment for Hodding, the biggest break of his young life. And Hodding had planned to assassinate him even if he had scored. Churchman thought about the potential for himself that would be within easy shooting range on the plaza below within a matter of minutes. The two men he had been assigned to destroy, the man who had set him up and, inadvertently, Carter Hodding himself. For a brief moment, Churchman contemplated a total massacre. He could return to New York, surprise Hodding and make a deal with him. But the thought made him chuckle softly to himself. Hodding would waste no time in attempting to end his career once again, and in New York City that would be an easy matter for the powerful man.

Churchman continued to run through the options when his thoughts were broken by the sound of approaching footsteps. He looked quickly to the source and saw the beam of a flashlight moving toward him from the far end of the bridge. The security guard had not seen him yet, but that was only a matter of seconds.

Churchman dropped to the cement and lay flat. He pulled the rifle down next to him and waited. The security guard walked slowly toward him, waving his flashlight back and forth across the bridge.

Churchman tensed and pulled himself up to a crawling position. When the guard, who was much smaller than himself, was within ten feet, Churchman sprung at him like a silent cat.

The security guard emitted a high-pitched shout, dropped his flashlight and fell tumbling backward. Churchman brought his knee up to the man's windpipe and looked directly into his face. The guard was white, and very old. His face twitched in fear and his eyes rolled.

"You be quiet," Churchman breathed, "and nothing going to happen."

The guard nodded.

"My knee's at your throat, and it won't take but one effort to destroy your windpipe."

The guard tried to talk, but Churchman's knee at his throat prevented him from doing much more than spewing forth a choked cry.

For a brief moment, Churchman felt panic. He did not want to kill the man, yet time was moving and any moment the meeting would begin on the plaza below. He knew if he released the old man he would cry out and blow his cover. The panic was created because Churchman did not want to kill him. The man had stepped into a situation at the wrong time, and Churchman felt anger at the fact that because of his poor timing he might have to die.

Lenny pulled the Ford to a halt on the street in front of the plaza. The space in front of the fountain was empty. It was five minutes past eleven.

"We keep riding till we see them," Lenny said in a hoarse whisper. He pulled away from the curb and moved slowly down the street. As they reached the end of the Arco lot, a large black Lincoln turned the corner and moved slowly past them toward the plaza. Lenny

213

caught a glimpse of four blacks inside the car.

"That got to be them," he said easily as he turned the corner and started around the block. Jason straightened up in his seat and put out his cigarette.

By the time they had circled the block, the Lincoln was parked in front of the plaza. Lenny pulled up behind it and turned off the engine. Four well-dressed black men stood in front of the fountain, watching as he and Jason got out of the car and walked slowly toward them.

Clinton Jones stepped forward, his three bodyguards standing at attention behind him. Jones smiled at the sight of the two young blacks. They were both good-looking men, with thin frames and a total lack of threatening posture. Jones immediately dropped his guard. He had figured right, he said to himself.

"The name is Clinton Jones."

Lenny nodded. "I'm Lenny, this is my partner, Jason."

Clinton Jones smiled, then lit a cigarette. "It ain't customary for me and my partners to do business like this, but this is an unusual situation."

Lenny waited, almost holding his breath. He wanted desperately to look up to the bridge spanning the seventh floor, but didn't dare. Instead, in a voice that was calm and even, he spoke. "I guess there ain't no shit about why we're here."

Clinton Jones nodded. "None at all, brother. Seems like things worked out strange. But I don't see why something positive can't come of all this shit, if you can dig where I'm coming from."

Lenny tried to smile, but the effort was a difficult one. "I think I can, my man," he said. "Me and Jason, we're tired of the shit and we want it cooled. Simple as that."

"I thought maybe you brothers might be thinking that way. I know I would if I was in your place, but I ain't," Clinton Jones added with a cold smile. "So, I think maybe we can talk."

"I hope so," Lenny replied.

"Carter Hodding," Jones began, "thinks you two are dead. I arranged that. I figured a couple of smart young bucks like yourselves might enjoy the opportunity of working with a real comer like myself. I figured Hodding blew his wad on a personal matter. That was a big mistake, the kind I don't make. So, I'm picking up the pieces and doing a little reorganizing."

Lenny listened, the words seemed to be tumbling from the tall, thin black man as if in a dream. Something had gone wrong, and Lenny was beginning to feel the nerves running wild throughout his body.

"Now," Jones continued, "the West Coast is a big place, and smart niggers like ourselves got all the opportunity in the world if we ready to grab hold. I think you two boys might be thinking along the same lines?"

"You're right on, brother," Lenny replied. "We come out here for that very reason."

Clinton Jones smiled. He was on top of the situation now, and knew that his master plan was working. He had the boys where he wanted them. He started to speak again, but as he opened his mouth a huge, cannon-like blast shattered the quiet peace of the plaza.

Lenny felt the concussion from the blast riddle his chest, then sensed something warm dripping down the front of his shirt. The top half of Clinton Jones' skull was plastered against his chest, the hair still intact and pieces of grey brain matter drooling from the bone.

The bullet had ripped his head open, thrown his body forward and face down onto the cement. It had been a perfect shot, Clinton Jones had died instantly.

Lenny and Jason reacted faster than Jones' bodyguards. Both men dropped to their knees and drew their weapons. They leveled their guns at the three men.

"Okay, cool it!" Lenny shouted. "You got but fifteen seconds to make a decision. Your man was a stupid, arrogant fool. Fact is, he's dead, and we taking over his operation. You come with us, you live and you get rich. You take revenge, and you get your fucking brains scattered like his."

Rufus looked at the body of Clinton Jones and smiled. It was a gruesome sight, with half his head blown away, but it still made him smile. The man was definitely a fool, Rufus decided.

"Ain't no need to get uptight, brother," Rufus said easily. "We all pros, and right now it looks like you got the action going down. We with you all the way . . . so long as you don't become no fool like Clinton here."

Lenny lowered his gun. "You dudes make it on over to 212 Palm Avenue, and we'll talk some more."

Rufus, Emory and Lincoln nodded to Lenny as they stepped over the body of Clinton Jones and headed for the Lincoln. Lenny turned to Jason and grinned. "For a minute there," he began, then stopped when he saw Churchman bolt from the lobby of the building and run toward them.

"Took your time, my man," Lenny chided.

Churchman smiled weakly. "Security guard. Man was frozen with fear. He up and died on me. A heart attack."

They ran to their car and sped away. There was still no sound of police sirens as they screamed onto the Santa Monica Freeway and headed toward Beverly Hills.

The house at 212 Palm Avenue was a Spanish style hacienda. It was located in a secluded section of Bel Air, high in the Hollywood Hills and away from the noises of the city. As Lenny pulled into the driveway, he checked out the cars in front. The black Lincoln, an old Pontiac, and three other cars which he did not recognize.

"What the shit?" Jason exclaimed as Lenny stopped the car in the huge circular driveway.

Lenny grinned. "Told you cats I had a little something for you. Say hello to your new home. This is where we handle our action from now on." Lenny jumped out of the car, with Jason and Churchman following.

Inside, the party was in full swing. Eight beautiful black girls danced in the center of the huge living room. Rufus, Emory and Lincoln leaned against the wall smoking cigarettes and appreciating the movements of the lithe young women. When Lenny entered the room, they turned toward him and grinned.

"You niggers with me?" Lenny shouted above the din of the music.

"Damn straight!" they replied in unison.

"Help yourself to anything that looks a might tasty," Lenny laughed.

Jason pulled his partner aside. "Got to admit, my man," Jason said with a broad grin, "we pulled one off this time."

"And this only the beginning, brother. Only the beginning."

Jason moved out onto the dance floor and took a beautiful, tall girl into his arms. Churchman, sitting alone on the couch, watched. Jason leaned over to the girl and whispered into her ear. She nodded and smiled, and Jason patted her affectionately on the rear. The girl made a beeline toward where Churchman was sitting and planted herself next to him. She said a few words to the homely man, and Churchman broke out into a wide grin.

Lenny stood off to the side of the living room and watched his people party. He appeared troubled and a little unsure of himself. A knock on the front door brought him out, and he moved quickly to answer it. Old Thadius stood with a big grin on his face, and a couple of bottles of wine in his hand. "How you doin'?" Thadius chortled.

Lenny put his arm around the old man, brought him into the house. And from out of the darkness stepped Wanda, looking radiant in a pink, clinging dress. She smiled, almost shyly, at Lenny.

"You're doing alright for yourself," she said with admiration.

"Just the beginning, baby. Just the beginning," Lenny said with a serious tone.

The main man of the house did not bother to introduce the white woman to any of his guests. Instead, he took her hand and led her up the stairs and into the master bedroom.

Lenny closed the door behind him. "Now," he began softly, "you a white woman in a black man's paradise." He moved quickly across to her and began undressing her. Wanda closed her eyes, a soft smile working its way across her full lips.

Death For Hire

Sugar Man's a high-powered underworld king who specializes in supplying the poison that the frustrated and needy pump into their veins. But the Assistant D.A.'s hot on his tail, willing and ready to put him and all the other dope dealers away.

Sugar Man doesn't want to make the hit, not when the courts are so lenient with juveniles. They can beat the raps that adults can't! So he recruits two teenagers, Tracy and Turtle, who idolize the underworld king and who cheerfully waste the prosecutor.

Unfortunately the bloody scene panics Tracy, who slams into a police car while trying to escape. Then the luckless youngblood has Sugar Man on his tail, as well as the black and white predators of the inner city jungle!

HOLLOWAY HOUSE PUBLISHING CO.
8060 MELROSE AVE., LOS ANGELES, CALIF. 90046

Gentlemen: I enclose _____ ☐ cash, ☐ check, ☐ money order, payment in full for books ordered. I understand that if I am not completely satisfied, I may return my order within 10 days for a complete refund. (Add 50c per order to cover postage. California residents add 6½% sales tax. Please allow three weeks for delivery.)

☐ **BH099, DEATH FOR HIRE, $2.25**

Name _____
Address _____
City _____ State _____ Zip _____

WHOREDAUGHTER

by CHARLIE AVERY HARRIS

The gripping novel of an incredibly evil, utterly deadly young girl...

Whoredaughter became a professional at the age of twelve. Whoredom was her heritage. Her grandmother had been a whore, her mother was a whore, and she neither knew nor wanted anything else. But it was bitterness and an all-encompassing hatred of men that drove her! ■ Foolishly, men tried to treat her as more than a ho— although disaster waited for all who fell in love with her. Even the rich and powerful white doctor who adopted her became a victim of her cruelty. Only one man could cope with Whoredaughter: Junius, the "Macking Gangster" who saw her for what she was, and forced her to the depths of degradation time after time. ■ Always, she bounced back, to continue blazing her trail of sex, intrigue and murder across the ghetto. Always— except that one last time...

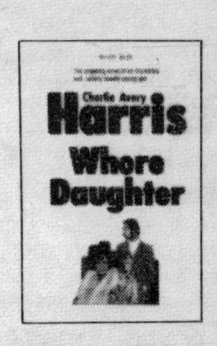

HOLLOWAY HOUSE PUBLISHING CO.
8060 MELROSE AVE., LOS ANGELES, CALIF. 90046

Gentlemen: I enclose _____ ☐ cash, ☐ check, ☐ money order, payment in full for books ordered. I understand that if I am not completely satisfied, I may return my order within 10 days for a complete refund. (Add 50¢ per order to cover postage. California residents add 6½% sales tax. Please allow three weeks for delivery.)

☐ **BH233, WHOREDAUGHTER, $2.25**

Name _____

Address _____

City _____ State _____ Zip _____

KENYATTA'S ESCAPE

by Donald Goines

WHITE RACIST COPS AND GHETTO DRUG PUSHERS TARGET OF GANGLORD KING'S BLOOD BATH!

■ Ganglord Kenyatta has two ambitions: cleaning the ghetto of all drug traffic and gunning down all the racist white cops! But a Black and white detective team, Benson and Ryan, have been on his tail all along.

■ They discover the location of his army's camp and, armed with tanks, bring a bloody Doomsday to his followers.

■ But Kenyatta hijacks a jet liner, ready to shoot his way into the biggest Black crime wave ever!

■ In KENYATTA'S ESCAPE author Donald Goines continues his story of the bloody, brutal world of crime started in CRIME PARTNERS and DEATH LIST. They're all back, for a coast-to-coast chase that will spell gripping adventure!

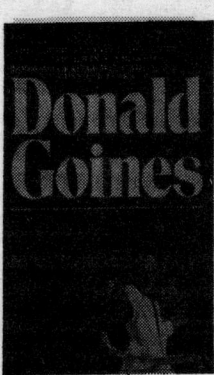

HOLLOWAY HOUSE PUBLISHING CO.
P.O. BOX 69804, LOS ANGELES, CALIFORNIA 90069

Gentlemen: I enclose _____ ☐ cash, ☐ check, ☐ money order, payment in full for books ordered. I understand that if I am not completely satisfied, I may return my order within 10 days for a complete refund. (Add 50¢ per order to cover postage. Calif. residents add 6% tax. Allow 3 weeks for delivery.)

☐ BH071, KENYATTA'S ESCAPE, $2.25

Name ....
Address ....
City .... State .... Zip ....

THE BLACK CONNECTION
by Randolph Harris
THE TRUE STORY OF THE BIGGEST HEROIN BATTLE IN CHICAGO HISTORY!

■ Oscar "Monk" Davis in a few wild and brutal years had built up a Black organization, widely heard of in the underground, often feared, and less often whispered about. He even gained the respect of the Mafia! ■ And in partnership with them Monk managed to get a grip on the heroin market in Chicago and Detroit. The politicians and Black police chief on the take never bothered him. But a teenage gang called "Black Angels" did. Complete with gruesome assasinations and Molotov cocktails! ■ And the big shipment comes. Two million dollars in the highest quality undiluted heroin! Shipped in from Jamaica to New York and Canada, then to the Black connection! ■ The action goes from a penitentiary to a Don's estate on Staten Island and then to Canada's Windsor Racetrack, as Federal agents and Interpol work against the clock to find a weak link in THE BLACK CONNECTION!

HOLLOWAY HOUSE PUBLISHING CO.
8060 MELROSE AVE., LOS ANGELES, CALIF. 90046

Gentlemen: I enclose _____ ☐ cash, ☐ check, ☐ money order, payment in full for books ordered. I understand that if I am not completely satisfied, I may return my order within 10 days for a complete refund. (Add 50c per order to cover postage. California residents add 6½% sales tax. Please allow three weeks for delivery.)

☐ BH077, THE BLACK CONNECTION, $2.25

Name _____
Address _____
City _____ State _____ Zip _____

The Life

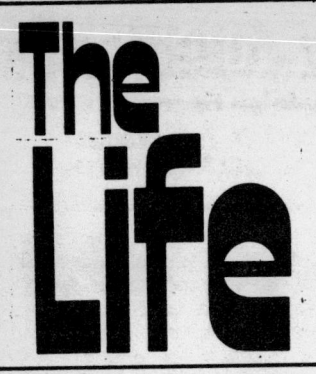

The Lore and Folk Poetry of the Black Hustler

FOLK POETRY/ On the streets of the inner city, in bars and "shooting galleries," poolrooms and prison yards, lively verses about the hustler are recited and learned. Here is an authentic collection of these folk poems that speak for the subculture known as "sporting life" or more recently as simply "the Life." Typically, they deal with those activities that characterize the Life: pimping and prostitution, the sale and use of narcotics, and a wide variety of confidence games.

Known as *toasts*, they are like jokes; no one knows who creates them, and everyone has his own version. Like all orally transmitted folk material, they are spread over a large area and may last a long time, and their form and content may change with each telling until they take on something of a communal character.

Each of the toasts is preceded by a headnote that evaluates, relates it to others in the collection, and describes the age and background of the performer. Included are a glossary and an index of titles and first lines.

HOLLOWAY HOUSE PUBLISHING CO.
8060 MELROSE AVE., LOS ANGELES, CALIF. 90046

Gentlemen: I enclose _____ ☐ cash, ☐ check, ☐ money order, payment in full for books ordered. I understand that if I am not completely satisfied, I may return my order within 10 days for a complete refund. (Add 50c per order to cover postage. California residents add 6½% sales tax. Please allow three weeks for delivery.)

☐ **BH205, THE LIFE, $2.25**

Name _____

Address _____

City _____ State _____ Zip _____

THE BLACK EXPERIENCE FROM HOLLOWAY HOUSE

★ ICEBERG SLIM

AIRTIGHT WILLIE & ME (BH031)	$2.25
NAKED SOUL OF ICEBERG SLIM (BH709)	2.75
PIMP: THE STORY OF MY LIFE (BH806)	2.95
LONG WHITE CON (BH030)	2.25
DEATH WISH (BH075)	2.25
TRICK BABY (BH807)	2.95
MAMA BLACK WIDOW (BH808)	2.95

★ DONALD GOINES

BLACK GIRL LOST (BH042)	$2.25
DADDY COOL (BH041)	2.25
ELDORADO RED (BH067)	2.25
STREET PLAYERS (BH034)	2.25
INNER CITY HOODLUM (BH033)	2.25
BLACK GANGSTER (BH028)	2.25
CRIME PARTNERS (BH029)	2.25
SWAMP MAN (BH026)	2.25
NEVER DIE ALONE (BH018)	2.25
WHITE MAN'S JUSTICE BLACK MAN'S GRIEF (BH027)	2.25
KENYATTA'S LAST HIT (BH024)	2.25
KENYATTA'S ESCAPE (BH071)	2.25
CRY REVENGE (BH069)	2.25
DEATH LIST (BH070)	2.25
WHORESON (BH046)	2.25
DOPEFIEND (BH044)	2.25
DONALD WRITES NO MORE (BH017)	2.25
(A Biography of Donald Goines by Eddie Stone)	

**AVAILABLE AT ALL BOOKSTORES OR ORDER FROM:
HOLLOWAY HOUSE, P.O. BOX 69804, LOS ANGELES, CA 90069
(NOTE: ENCLOSE 50¢ PER BOOK TO COVER POSTAGE.
CALIFORNIA RESIDENTS ADD 6½% SALES TAX.)**